Above Average: The Journey

Phil Thompson

Above Average: The Journey

Copyright © 2024 by Phil Thompson

All Rights Reserved

No part of this book may be reproduced or transmitted in any form or by any means, electronic or mechanical, including photocopying, recording, or by any information storage and retrieval system without the written permission of the author, except where permitted by law.

This book is dedicated to all those that worked for years in their field and were above average, but seldom recognized for doing the little things to make those around them better. To those that came to work every day, never complained but did their job with a positive attitude, and made valuable contributions to those they worked with. This book is dedicated to all the Above Average individuals today who are the true heroes in the world today!

Table of Contents

Introduction

Case Study – 01-00799903 – Above Average

Background

- Planet: Earth
- Cultural background: The United States of America

Identify 100 individuals, an equal number of males and females, from all walks of life. These individuals should all have been above average in their areas of employment. Characteristics include:

- Always there and on time, even early in most cases.
- Solid work ethic and is not afraid to spend extra time to make sure something gets done.
- Develops relationships with others that are real and authentic.
- Communicates well and listens to understand.
- Gets a lot of information and input before they make decisions.
- Finds time to have "balance" in their lives.

- Doesn't have to get credit for things that are done well.

These individuals will come from a variety of places in the United States, have different backgrounds, and have a number of varied beliefs and values that will influence their decisions throughout this study.

The intent of this study is to see how an above-average group of individuals will interact and deal with a variety of tasks and problems they will face in a completely foreign environment. These tasks and problems will include:

Overall observations made throughout the Case Study:

- Communicating effectively with a variety of individuals in a new and different environment.
- Developing relationships with individuals, they don't know when they are in a unique setting.
- Ability to form some type of cohesive society that can be self-sufficient and self-sustaining.
- Ability to respond to change and show adaptability and flexibility.
- Ability to handle and deal with conflict.
- Ability to identify differences in relationships based on a variety of personality types.

Observations made due to specific circumstances the individuals are placed in:

- Adjust to a completely different environment with no knowledge of how they got there or why they were chosen to be there.
- Deal with the concept of all individuals being assigned a number and see what it leads to in the overall development of their community.
- Identify how this group of individuals will deal with an above-average sociopath that poses a threat to all the members of the community.

Types of methods that will be used to collect information:

- Case Study
- Observation
- Number of survivors

PHASE I

Chapter One: What the heck is going on??

I woke up, regained consciousness, or, well, I'm not really sure what happened, but from what I could tell I was on an island or in some type of tropical location. I had on a pair of cotton, gray sweat shorts and a white T-shirt that both had the #98 in big, bold print on them. No shoes, no socks, just my bare feet, and I was lying under a tree in the sand.

It was hot and humid; my body was sweaty, and my shirt was sticking to my body. When I moved, sweat started dripping from me; it was uncomfortable, and I could tell I wasn't in Wyoming anymore. When I looked around, all I could see were palm trees, ferns, and lush vegetation. It was a deep green and dotted with beautiful colors from the flowers that were blooming throughout the jungle.

I could hear what sounded like waves crashing on the beach and the noises from the various insects that inhabited this place. My wife and I enjoyed going to beautiful beaches and tropical locations and had just been to Jamaica, and everything that I was sensing reminded me of a tropical destination.

I'm not sure where I was and could not remember what I had been doing before I found myself in these circumstances. I had no idea where I was, no clue how I got there, and was completely befuddled by the whole experience. As I continued to observe the area around me, I got even more confused. I just couldn't wrap my brain around where I was or how I could have got here.

The last thing I remember was that I had just retired from over 40 years in the educational arena. The previous day, my wife had given me flight training on a small airplane, and I was going to try to get my flying license over the next few months.

Now, I was in a tropical setting and had no idea where I was or how I got there. I was trying to get more acclimated to my new surroundings and get a better understanding of where I might be. It seemed like it was dusk, the sun was setting, and it was getting dark when suddenly, I heard a scream.

"Help me, help me!" Coming from the beach.

I quickly got up and ran from the trees that surrounded me. An athletic-looking individual, tan and fit, around 6'2", and a young lady on the ground under his gaze, looking very scared and screaming for help.

She continued, "Someone help me," and she had a terrified, confused look on her face.

I ran out and yelled in my best principal voice, "Hey! What's going on here?"

I startled them, and they both stopped and stared at me. The young lady tried to squirm away and said, "Thank God! I need help!"

The man looked at me angrily and told me, "Get the hell out of here; this is none of your business!"

I responded, "Let's talk about this."

The man stopped his advances on her and stepped in my direction. I had been a principal long enough to know that something was not right, but was unsure what was going on and just wanted to try to figure this out.

The man came at me and repeated, "Get the hell out of here, or I'll kick your ass!" He seemed upset and moved forward aggressively.

I said, "I'm just trying to find out what is going on."

At that point, he threw a punch that caught me squarely in the jaw and then followed it with a roundhouse kick that knocked me to the ground. I have to tell you, I broke up a number of fights in my day, but as a principal, you have a certain "power," and most students respect that, and you didn't get hit.

The only time I can remember getting hit was when I had broken up a girl fight. They were the most intense, and boys tended to posture more than fight when girls flat got after it, pulling hair and scratching. I had to literally box out one of the girls as they continued to swing and claw at each other with me getting hit a number of times with errant blows until another staff member pulled one of the girls away.

I was completely stunned; I had never really been hit before, and all those things you see in the movies and on TV don't truly show how much something like that hurts. I lay on the ground, and the man hovered over me and said, "Mind your own business."

I tried to say something but couldn't. He then gave me a good solid kick to the ribs and repeated, "Get the hell out of here!"

The girl started to move away and head out into the water while he focused on me. I noticed this and again started to try to engage the man in a conversation about what was going on. "What did I do?"

He became more irritated and started to move aggressively towards me. I was still pretty much in shock but had gained some strength back, and this time, when he went to kick me, I blocked it and gave a quick jab to his face. I doubt it hurt him; in fact, it probably just made him madder. Then I quickly moved into the water, hoping it would give me some type of advantage and I would be in a position to at least help the young lady get away.

My face was bleeding, I think he had broken my nose, and I was having trouble breathing and was prepared to get hammered when he stopped proceeding. I continued to move farther back into the water and was surprised when the man glared at me but did not come after me.

For the first time, I realized the man had on the exact same thing I did, but he had the number #6 on his white t-shirt. I continued to move out to talk to the young lady as the man kept close watch from the beach.

She quickly introduced herself, "I'm Jessica Morgan. Thanks for helping me."

She proceeded to tell me, "I went to sleep last night, then this morning I just seemed to be "planted" on this island. I was dazed, confused, and trying to figure out what was going on when this angry guy surprised me."

She had instinctively yelled for help when the situation had escalated, with the man getting more and more aggressive until I arrived.

As we talked, it was getting dark, and I told Jessica, "Move out farther into the water, then get as low as possible and swim along the shore until you're out of sight. I'll try to distract him." I continued, "When you get out of sight, sneak out of the water and try to find a safe place for the night."

In the morning, I told her to find the biggest tree she could find, and I would try to meet her there and figure out what was going on.

After finishing my talk with Jessica, I went back to have a conversation with the man I had the altercation with. As a principal, I always found that after giving time to de-escalate a situation, sometimes you could talk and find out what was going on, and you could accomplish a lot.

I quickly found this wasn't the case. When I returned, he was madder than ever and started yelling, "I'm going to kick your ass, get out of the water and fight like a man!"

I tried to reason with him but found that the more I stayed in the water, the madder he got. The amazing thing was that as mad as he was, he would still not enter the water to get me. I stayed hip-deep in the water and continued to try to distract him so Jessica could get away. I found that trying to have a reasonable conversation with an individual who would kill me if he got the chance was a challenging task, but it did give Jessica the chance to get away.

It continued to get dark, and after about 20 minutes of his angrily yelling at me and calling me some pretty nasty names, I decided to go out into the water and see how he would respond. As I moved out into the water, he started to get tired and lose interest in pursuing me.

I found the water had some medicinal effect on my body, but I still had trouble breathing, and my face and ribs hurt badly. I was pretty sure he couldn't see me, and I hoped I could wait him out and eventually get out of the water and look for a safe place to spend the night, then look for Jessica and try to figure out what was happening.

After what seemed like a couple of hours, I moved on to the beach and hurried into the trees. I felt terrible and couldn't help thinking about the last few hours. I was on some type of tropical island and had just been beaten up by someone who was wearing the exact same clothes that I had on but had the #6 on his white T-shirt.

From what I could tell, he was attacking a young lady who, after I had thought about it, was kinda cute, and I had the feeling I had seen her somewhere before. I had helped her escape and was supposed to meet up with her tomorrow at the largest tree we could find. As I thought it over, it was probably not the best plan one could come up with, and we would have to see if there were any big trees tomorrow when it was light.

None of this made sense, and the more I thought about it, I was hoping it was a bad dream and I would wake up tomorrow and look forward to golfing nine holes with my son. But I couldn't help getting the feeling that my face and ribs were not part of a bad dream, more like a nightmare and one that might continue for some time.

14

Chapter Two: Survival

I had a lot of trouble sleeping due to the pain, but after the day I had, I think the exhaustion just took over. When I woke up, I realized it wasn't a bad dream. I was still somewhere where it was hot and humid, there was a beach, and I hurt like hell. My mind automatically went to the events of the previous day; what the heck happened, and what was going on? My ribs and the black and blue around my nose and eyes told me that what I remembered actually happened, and the #98 on my shirt was still there. I knew I needed to get up and move around. I couldn't just lay there and feel sorry for myself. I was a little scared that #6 would be around, but if I stayed near the beach, I could just get in the water and, if last night was any indication, he wouldn't come after me.

I also had planned with Jessica to try to meet up, and maybe she had some answers. I got up and did some exercise and yoga. I had been trying to stretch, work on my balance, and stay fit as I got older, and I hoped by continuing some of these habits, I could add some normalcy to all the confusion I was experiencing.

I still hurt, but I decided to try to figure out what the heck was going on and what my next steps needed to be to. I was pretty sure staying alive was my #1 priority. After that, I figured I needed to find some fresh water and food and see if I could get back to my wife and family in Wyoming.

I walked out to the beach and surveyed where I was. It was a beautiful place; it had a pristine beach with white, soft sand, lots of trees, and big, majestic mountains in the background. I have been to Maui a couple of times, and this place was comparable in every way. Just how did I get here, and where was here?

As I looked back into the trees, I looked for the tallest tree I could find, and not one stood out; instead, there were hundreds of tall trees, and I didn't know whether Jessica had gone north or south, east or west, the night before.

I didn't want to just start yelling her name because #6 might be around, and after last night, I didn't feel like I wanted to get into another altercation with him. I went to a couple of different trees and quietly yelled, "Hey Jessica," but didn't get a response.

I went out and took a dip in the water. It seemed to help my pain last night, and I hoped it could offer some type of relief for the aches and pain I was suffering. The sand and water were great, and I started to feel a little better.

Then, I just sat down to think about things. This was crazy, and I had no idea what I was going to do; I was alone and clueless about what was going on in my life right now. I had always had a routine. I knew what I was doing, I enjoyed it, and for over 40 years, I had done my job. Whether it be coaching, teaching, or administrating, I have done it well. As a parent, I had raised two great kids and had developed a life I was looking forward to when I retired. Now all I could think of was "What the Hell?" has happened!!!

I had watched enough "Naked and Afraid" episodes to know I had to find water, shelter, and eventually food. I looked around carefully to see if there were any cameras around. I was hoping this was a cruel joke, and I was on a new reality show, but no such luck. So, I decided to head inland and look for drinkable water and a good place to build a camp. Hopefully, I could find a lake that had drinkable water and fish I could catch to provide food.

I couldn't tell for sure, but at least for now, I didn't see any type of wildlife, and I was sure there would be some type of fruit or vegetables I could use for my nutritional needs. I figured it was about 2 pm and decided to start a hike into the island core in hopes of finding things that would provide the necessary building blocks for survival.

My survival skills consisted of finding a sturdy stick to make a spear and utilizing it to work my way through a dense forest and ward off any snakes or wildlife I might encounter. I wanted to find a place that would be hard for others to get to and that I could not leave too much of a trail to be followed. After dealing with #6, I was scared that others on the island, if there were any other people, may have similar temperaments, and I wanted to get my bearings before I meant anyone else.

I would identify a point I wanted to get to that was on higher ground and keep my eye on that in hopes of not getting lost or ending up going in circles. I spent a lot of time identifying key landmarks and mentally tracking where I had been and where I was going. By six o'clock, I had hiked about, maybe two miles, and stumbled on a lake that seemed like a great spot to build a camp. The hike had been difficult. As far as I could tell, no one had ever been through the thick forest I had just come through, and it had been an arduous task to work my way up to this particular sight.

The whole time, I continued to pinch myself and try to convince myself to wake up. When I was convinced this was real, I kept trying to figure out what was happening and what I was going to have to do to survive.

I couldn't stop thinking about my life before today, "What was my wife thinking?" I'd been missing for two days now, and she had to be wondering where I was. I started to get more and more anxious and worried about what I needed to do to get back to her and my family.

I had grown up in the country on a farm, and occasionally, my parents would allow us to camp out in a small thicket we had in the pasture. We would all act like we were outdoorsmen and spend the night outside with some friends. Invariably, we realized that camping wasn't all it was cracked up to be, and after we turned 15, we never had the desire to rough it anymore, but those experiences provided some insight into what I needed to do here to be successful. Some of my friends had a camping experience, and those tricks, building a fire, making a shelter, and fishing, they had used were coming in handy.

That evening, I built a makeshift bed with tree branches and leaves and worked to build a fire. It wasn't the best sleep I've ever had, but each night, I continued to improve my living arrangements and develop better tools and amenities to help me make this place a home. This allowed me to work on building my camp so that I pretty much forgot about why I was here or where I was. I simply worked to make sure while I was here, I would be as safe and secure as possible.

I also had been having success in finding food in the form of fruits and vegetables and found the island has a decent number of resources that could sustain a person living here. I found some apples, berries, and other various vegetables and had success catching some fish from the nearby lake. Although a little hungry, I've been able to forage enough food to not be uncomfortable.

Not only was I building my camp and finding food, but I was also getting up every morning and walking and surveying the land around my campsite, mapping out the different landmarks around, and getting the "lay of the land." It does remind me of the islands I've visited, and I'm starting to get a good understanding of the terrain I'm living in and how to navigate it successfully.

The time has also given me a chance to get through the beating I had taken, and I realized that the aches and pains that I had were no longer as bad; in fact, after day number three, I could breathe fine, and when I looked in the lake, didn't see the black and blue marks on my face. In fact, I seemed to have more energy, and the training I was doing seemed to be having a more positive effect on my overall health. I wasn't sure, but I think you feel broken ribs and bruises on your face longer than three days, but in my case, I was feeling pretty chipper.

My campsite was becoming homey, and I feel pretty good about the shelter I have developed. The shelter has room for a decent-sized "bed" that was made of palm leaves and dried leaves. I added anything soft that I could find to make the bed as comfortable as possible. I had elevated it using bamboo, and it helped with keeping the bugs out when I was trying to sleep. It had a thatched roof that kept the bed dry when it rained and had enough room that I was comfortable when I was in it. The weather is nice, although it does get a little cold at night. As I find more resources in the area and as I continue to be resilient and improve upon the things I have established, it is becoming more of a home.

I'm not sure, but I think it's been three weeks since I arrived at this tropical destination. But I'm starting to hunker down and develop some strong routines. I don't know what they will lead to or if I'll ever see a benefit from them, but I do know they keep me busy, and I am making progress on the things I want to do.

Chapter Three: #98 = Drew

I had been a teacher and coach for 27 years, then moved on to be a principal for 16 years, and had just completed a job as a principal for a decent-sized high school in Wyoming. Overall, I was satisfied with my 40 years in education. I have been successful in working with a variety of students over the years. I had enjoyed teaching and coaching and had developed great relationships with students who had been in my classes. I had some successful basketball teams and still kept in touch with a number of my players and students. As a principal, I worked with a challenging group of students but had found ways to help them. Overall, we had developed a good team of teachers. The students were good kids who had learned what it took to be successful. Not all took advantage of that, but overall, if I were being honest, I would say I had been an above-average leader who cared for and found ways to support the people I worked with. I had, through 40 years in the public school arena, played a variety of roles, learned how to be patient and flexible, and get the most out of the people I worked with.

I had forged very good relationships with the staff, the students genuinely respected me, and I continually dealt with a myriad of problems from the parents. Overall, I felt that my job was a challenge, and I can honestly say I enjoyed most aspects of it and had become very good at navigating all that went along with it. I truly believe it was a very difficult job, but had learned that by surrounding yourself with good people, people you could trust, and giving them the responsibility and tools to do their job, it became easier, and you got more accomplished. I was always willing to listen to staff, students, and parents and had a great group of assistants who took the initiative and had great ideas to help our kids.

I was always there, never missed a day unless deathly ill, made sure I did my job effectively, and communicated with the students, staff, and parents to try to continue to find ways to help the school and community. I listened to understand, gathered as much input as possible to make informed choices, and always tried to look at the big picture when making decisions that would impact our school and students positively.

The last quality I felt was imperative to any position was to always see the positive in things. Over my career, I have seen too many people become bitter and negative toward their jobs and the people they worked with. It was like a cancer, and I had told myself that if I became that person, I would quit and look for something else to do. I wasn't at that stage yet, but I wanted to make sure I left feeling good about my career and the people I worked with. I took every experience and tried to learn from them, even if they sucked at the time.

I had retired and was looking forward to spending my next 10-15 years exploring things that I had never had the time to do in the past. I had a bucket list of things I was going to pursue; in fact, I remembered I had just ridden a scooter and hopped on a paddle board in Jamaica for the first time and was working on improving my balance because I had watched a reel that said that was key to staying healthy and fit as you got older. Overall, I was in pretty good health. I had taken care of myself over the years, other than having an occasional Mountain Dew, Hostess cupcake (my guilty pleasures), and beer and pizza on weekends. I wasn't perfect, but I was in pretty good physical condition. I was 6' tall, with thinning gray hair, around 215 pounds, and a bit of a dad bod, but overall, I thought I looked OK for being 64. I was going to start taking flying lessons at a small local airport and was embracing this whole retirement thing and trying to stay healthy as long as I could.

Chapter Four: Time to get out amongst 'em

According to my records, I have been here for seventeen days and have not seen anyone else. I had created a sundial to track approximate times and kept track of the days I had been "planted" on a tree located nearby. I had settled into a routine that included getting up every morning when the sun came up and swimming two lengths of the lake. I figure, about a half mile across, so around three miles.

I didn't start with that; I was lucky to make it from one side to the other, but every five days, I try to increase the length I swim. I then do some yoga, stretching and have been trying to self-teach myself how to become a better fighter, just in case I meet #6 again. This must look amusing if anyone could see it because I've never boxed, done any martial arts, or actually fought, but I'm trying to use all the moves I've seen on TV that seem to make sense.

After that, I took time to develop some weapons. I have made a couple of spears, a solid bat-like apparatus that I have been working on using as a tool to ward off any animals or other things I might come into contact with. I think it is kind of weird, but I have seen no evidence of any wildlife other than hens, ducks, and some other funky-looking birds. I have started to develop a bow and arrow, but that is proving harder to do than I thought it would.

These two activities took till about 1 o'clock to complete, and then I took the next part of the day to explore my surroundings and see what I could find that might help me survive the next few weeks. I feel good I picked an area that was hard to get to and had a lot of trees and forestry that made it feel secure. I'm pretty sure no one else could find me unless they were really looking for me. Then, every evening, I go out and look for food and other forms of sustenance to give me the energy I need to go through my daily routine.

The first seventeen days, I have stayed close to my home camp and have not been willing to head down near the beach, instead choosing to fortify my area and become more physically capable of defending myself in case something out there exists that could put me in danger. I guess I'm satisfying Physiological and Safety and Security needs based on Maslow's Hierarchy of needs. I have always tried to use common sense in most of my life struggles and routines. I have located some trees in the area and am working on seeing how fast I can climb them in case of a threat. I have even placed some spears up in the trees - just in case.

I try to think of what challenges I will face in this new environment and incorporate those into my daily routines. I'm not sure what challenges are out there, but figure that self-preservation and being ready for any surprises that might await me are worth trying to prepare for in my daily routines.

Staying healthy and fit seems like a rational idea to make it until I figure out what is going on. I will admit my thoughts often go out to Jessica and wonder if she is surviving, and how great it would be if I happened to run into her. I'm just not sure how that is going to happen, and I hope that she is as resilient as I am and has been successful in navigating this new place and staying safe and secure.

One of my biggest distractions is when I think back to before I got here. I had a great life. My wife and I had just come back from a great vacation in Jamaica. I had two new granddaughters, ages one and four, that we enjoyed visiting and having them come stay with us. It was hard not to think about how they were doing and if they wondered where I was and where I had gone. I found that if I started thinking about the past, it was hard to concentrate and invariably got me thinking about how I got here and where I was. The more I kept busy, the more productive I could be and get things done. I was figuring things out in this new land but still had a lot of questions that, no matter how hard I tried, just didn't make any sense at all.

Today is day 18, and I'm determined to look for Jessica and see if there is anyone on this island. I have packed some weapons, water, and food to take a two-to-three-day journey and am in explorer mode. I have made six pairs of sandals. I don't have TV or video games, and at night, I sit down and work on developing sandals that don't hurt your feet. I know it sounds simple, but I have found, after walking all the miles I have, it is nice to have a comfortable pair of sandals. I worked to make a couple of pairs and figured out that if I ran into someone, it might be nice to have a gift to offer as a way to break the ice, so to speak. Hopefully, I'm not the only person in this new place, and If I can find someone else, maybe they can explain what is going on.

I hope I don't meet up with #6 or anyone else who would be hostile, but what the hell? I've got to see what's out there. My plan is to make as much noise as possible, have a clear destination, mark my trail for future reference, and see what is going on in my new world. After 17 days, I will admit that I'm a little lonely and would like to move on to the next of Maslow's Needs, that of relationships and social-emotional stability. If I continue to talk to myself,

I'm afraid I'll piss myself off; then, who will I have to talk to? I'm heading to the beach to try to find out if more people exist, and if they do, what are the next steps we need to take to get off this island?

I've traveled probably a mile and made as much noise as possible, hoping that if someone hears me, they will call out and make contact. Again, I believe there must be other people, and I'm even willing to run into #6 and try to work things out.

I'm cutting a trail and marking my path when suddenly, I hear something rustling ahead. I have my bat ready to defend and call out to see if it is an animal or hoping someone will call out.

I call out, "Is anyone out there?"

Suddenly, I am surrounded by five individuals. Three women and two men. It is an interesting mix of backgrounds: an individual that appears to be Asian, a Latino, and what looks to be an individual of Middle Eastern descent, along with two white males. They have primitive weapons, seem curious, and don't seem to be a threat. The first thing I notice is they all have white T-shirts and gray shorts with numbers on them.

I hold out my sandals and say, "Anyone need some shoes? I've got a couple of free pairs."

It sounds dumb, but how do you introduce yourself to someone you don't know in a place you know nothing about?

It gets a smile from four of them, and the other one, an older white male, who seems a little high-strung anyways, just stares at me and says, "Are they comfortable?"

We relax a little, and they start to introduce themselves.

Kathy, #87, is a professional hairdresser and lives in Waco, Texas.

Tanver, #26, is a scientist who specializes in environmental issues from San Diego, California.

Kim, #18, is a registered nurse who has the friendliest smile and seems to be a positive, enthusiastic young lady who genuinely is glad to see me.

The two males introduce themselves as Bob, #74, a Real Estate agent from Bend, Oregon, and Brodie, #55, the serious one is military, a recruiting instructor from Quantico, Virginia.

Once the ice is broken, we all start to ask questions, none that anyone can answer.

Kim asks, "Do you know where we are at?"

Bob asks, "How did you get here?"

Tanver asks, "Do you know why we are here?"

Everyone offers possible explanations, but when all is said and done, we all agree no one has any solid answers, and we just talk. They seem to enjoy having someone new to talk to, and I'm just glad to realize I'm not the only one on this island. We talk about the different lives we had before we were "planted" and explore if we might have some common themes that might connect us.

I mention my age and explain, "I'm 64, and since I've been on the island, I feel really good and am feeling younger every day."

Kim says, "I feel good too. The island seems really good for my skin and complexion; the island seems to be good for our health."

Even Brodie chimes in, "Yeah, my joints and bones don't ache like they did back home."

I just listen for the next few minutes; over the years, I have learned the best communication strategy is to listen and let everyone else have the chance to talk. I've found this practice allows me to learn a lot more about people, and people respect the opportunity to talk and share. I've also found by listening, you can find out a lot about the personality of the people you are interacting with, especially before you really know someone.

When Brodie talks, he speaks clearly and says, "I was in the military, and it has helped me be ready for something like this." He explains he was on training exercises, and this reminds him of a training exercise.

The more we talked, the more I learned about my new friends. First, they were all educated and good at what they did. Bob was everything you would expect from a real estate agent. He was affable, well-spoken, and just seemed like a nice guy.

The same with Brodie. He'd been involved in the Gulf War and had spent two tours in Iraq. He was a tad cynical but had a true understanding of how to survive and the skills necessary to deal with the uncertainty we had stumbled into.

The females were also smart and articulate and had a good grasp of their skills and how they could be used in this unusual situation.

Kim was everything I thought when she talked; you could tell she loved being a nurse and loved helping others. Her warm, positive vibe could be seen in all her interactions with the rest of the people in her group.

Tanver and Kathy both seemed nice and had similar traits when it came to their work and the jobs they had. You could tell Tanver when she mentioned how "the terrain was tropical and supported a variety of plant and animal species that we could live on for a long time," ~~she~~ knew what she was talking about.

They all had been respected in their different communities and, although confused, seemed ready to tackle the new challenges they faced here.

The discussion was nice, and we got to know each other; it was comforting to know there were others on the island that I could communicate with and work with to make this a pleasant experience while it lasted.

As the discussion continued, Brodie asked a question, "What's with the numbers on our shirts?"

I think all of us were wondering, but the other issues were more pressing. It was an innocent question, but it got us thinking. Kim had the lowest number, #18; I had the highest, #98.

We had all come into contact with seven different individuals, and all had a T-shirt with numbers between 6 and 98. I wasn't sure what those numbers meant, but I felt there had to be a reason, but responded with, "Damned if I know, but we've got bigger things to worry about, and I'm more worried about finding out why we're here and how to get back home."

Everyone agreed, and they invited me to spend the night in their camp, which I thought was a nice gesture, and headed over to their place for the rest of the evening.

It was an organized camp with everything they needed to survive, and they even had a smokehouse for fish and game that they had caught. I quickly found out that this group could handle the challenging situation they had been thrust into and seemed to do it better as a team. I thought I'd wait till morning and explore what options I should choose concerning the direction I wanted to go in the future.

I was up with the sun and met Brodie and Kim out in an open area, having some breakfast and chatting. I sat down, and they offered me some smoked fish and water. It tasted good and was different from what I had been eating every morning for the last three weeks.

I really liked this camp but had decided I was going to continue my exploration.

I said, "Thanks for the chance to talk with other people. It's nice to know I'm not the only one on this island."

Then, I went on to let them know how much I appreciated the great breakfast. I told them, "I have marked the trail each day and will make a trailhead here and be a frequent visitor."

Kim walked with me for a few hundred yards and made it a point to say, "It was great to see you on the island, and I hope you'll come back and visit."

She shared that she was concerned and trying to get as many people as possible to band together. She thought it was a good idea and that she strongly believed the more we worked together, the better this situation would be.

We gave a brief hug, and I started my journey for the day with a strong, positive feeling about the group I just met and what the next few days might bring.

Chapter Five: Anybody else out there?

I had been exploring for three days after meeting with Kim and her friends and was ready to head home. I had seen some beautiful terrain but had not come across any more people. I was making my normal loud swath through the forest when I got a strange feeling that I was being watched. I couldn't put my finger on it, but I had a feeling, and it was sort of creepy. I continued to move through the trees and decided to go into stealth mode (remember, I had been practicing different ninja moves earlier). I was moving loudly when suddenly, I took a quick right, then a quick left and ran through a thicket and stopped and just hid. I didn't move. I figured I'd sit there for a while, and if nothing happened, I had just made a couple of quick moves for fun and possible future reference.

As I sat, I heard some rustling and heard a couple of voices. There were three of them, as far as I could tell, and they were giving each other signals to where they thought I might be. They had clubs and were beating through the thicket I had just passed through. They had split up and were communicating but had split far enough apart that they had lost line of site.

One of the individuals was getting closer, but I had practiced for a situation like this and surprised him before he could say anything. Luckily, he was not well equipped to handle my surprise attack, and I disarmed him, whispered, "Shut up!" and threatened him with my bat.

The other two continued to yell for him to respond, and I quickly tried to assess the situation. I decided that if they wanted to hurt me, they could, but in most of the interactions, the people I had met had been basically good people, other than #6, and I put my bat down and told him to yell for his associates and let them know I met no harm.

He yelled out, "Over here!" and his buddies came rushing to his aid.

His buddies came rushing over and demanded, "Who are you, and what are you doing here?"

They gave me the third degree about running from them, then attacking their friend.

I responded, "I wasn't sure what to expect and felt I was being watched and feel I acted appropriately."

I continued to relate to them;, which I had been exploring for a couple of days, and the other group I had communicated with had been great to talk to. We found out a lot by simply having discussions and communicating.

A guy named Don, who seemed to be the leader, started to calm down and asked, "Where did you come from, and how many other guys have you met?"

We started to have a civil conversation. This group of three men had a completely different demeanor from the other group I had visited. They reminded me of my redneck buddies I grew up with in Ohio. Great guys who would give you the shirt off their back, but at the same time, they are a little wary of outsiders and a little stuck in their ways.

Don, #48, was a farm kid. He had taken over for his dad on the ranch in South Dakota and had made it into a successful operation by incorporating hard work and technology. He had found ways to streamline the breeding process for his cattle and had a prime Hereford Ranch that ran over 1000 head of cattle for beef production.

Jessie, #79, was a world-class fisherman. He bragged, "I've won fishing tournaments all over the country and have a coupla endorsement deals." He was a well-known fisherman and was known for his tenacity and willingness to do whatever it took to catch the most and biggest fish in the pond.

#92, Louis was a little bit of a fish out of water with these two. He was an "investment guy," his words, not mine. He told me, "I made a bunch of money in securities, but the stress was unbelievable," but gave no particulars and talked in broad generalizations that made me wonder if he really knew what he was talking about.

Between the three of them, we had a nice talk and connected on a number of different levels. Both Don and Jessie were salt-of-the-earth type of guys, farm kids who were raised with good old-fashioned values and respect for the land and what it produces. I can't put my finger on it, but Louis didn't fit and seemed to be trying too hard to fit in. The more we talked, the more I was convinced that Louis had convinced Don and Jessie to have some fun with me. I thought it was funny that Louis was the one I had surprised. I don't think I could have done that to the other two.

As a principal, I had to sort through a lot of shit. When there was a fight, I had to really listen and get all the input I could before I would make a decision. When parents had a concern about teachers and the treatment of their kids, I had to hear what parents said and diplomatically talk to the teacher and student. I have got pretty good at spotting bullshit over the years, and I call it a gut feeling. Louis seemed to be full of it.

I didn't rush to judgment, and over the years, I've learned it takes time to get to know people. My running joke with my staff is that I really don't know a person until I've been through some rough times and see how they deal with it; that usually takes about two years. Too many times, I've met someone new that is great, but after a few years, they're not the person I thought they were, and they often were selling me a load of crap for their benefit and couldn't always be trusted. I'd give Louis every chance in the future, but I just had a feeling I'd met his kind before, and it hadn't ended well.

That night, we all told stories about growing up on the farm and the way we were raised. It took me back to when I was a kid on the farm and a much simpler time, a time that was a lot more like this place than the world I had left. As the evening progressed, there was no doubt that Jessie was a storyteller. He had a lot of tall tales and told some great fish stories.

He explained, "I'm the best fisherman in the land and have more trophies than anyone in North America." We all doubted the voracity of his story, but we didn't have any information to argue. We all figured he was like every fisherman who always told us about the big one that got away.

Don and Jessie were going to be a must for any team we would develop to be successful in this new world. Their farm and fishing smarts were invaluable in the environment we were in, and they could help us make sure we were prepared for hard times as far as food and shelter that might come up in the future. How the two of them ended up together was a great coincidence, and I knew I had two friends I could trust. Louis, I don't want to pass judgment too quickly, but I feel I am a good judge of character, and I have some concerns that I'll need to address before I can call him a trusted friend.

The next morning, we said our goodbyes, and I made sure to identify major sights to landmark these guys' locations. I feel we had a solid connection, and I hoped that when I left, Don and Jessie felt the same, no matter what Louis thought or told them.

Before I left, we talked about when planting season might be. It seemed to be a tropical climate, and Jessie, Don, and I decided that I would try to come back in about two weeks. We could try to break new ground and prepare it for planting. It would be hard work, but the soil seemed fertile, and we felt the sooner we could plant some crops, the better.

I felt good about the two groups I had met while exploring. I figured it would just be a matter of time until I came back down and joined forces with one of them. I went back to my camp and was determined to come up with a plan to try to get the proper things in place to help all the people I had come into contact with be successful in this new world, even #6, if we were to meet again.

42

Chapter Six: Who's going to lead?

According to my homemade sundial, I got back to camp around 6:00 pm on day #23. I was just settling down, looking forward to some downtime, and getting back into my routines when I heard a strange sound. I stopped and listened and again heard a loud horn type of sound. At first, I thought it might be a ship's horn and my questions would be answered, but the more I listened, my mind went back to "Lord of the Flies," a book I had read in high school and had continued to teach when I taught Sociology class. The noise reminded me of the noise a conch makes, and someone was signaling.

Instinctively, I got up and started to follow the sound. It was coming from the beach, and if I heard it, anyone else in the vicinity would also hear it and be intrigued by who was making it, what they wanted, and who would show up. It took me 15-20 minutes to get from my camp to the beach, and when I did, I was flabbergasted. There were over 50 people on the beach. A few I had encountered, but most I had never seen and wondered where they had been hiding.

The man who was blowing the conch was none other than good old #6. He had all the others gathering around him and looking to him for direction. I thought, *"Oh shit, this isn't going to go well."*

My thoughts immediately went back to Ralph and Jack, good versus evil. I just hoped I wasn't going to be Piggy, and I could see the man with the conch, at least for tonight, was the man with the power.

As the people gathered, I hunkered down and stayed out of sight. I had learned to listen and not get involved. Most of the individuals I encountered were bright, articulate individuals, and hopefully, we would have great discussions, figure out some things, and develop a plan to get us back to our normal lives. "The Lord of the Flies" was just a book about kids; we were adults that, although confused, were looking for answers and were smart enough to sort through the shit and find credible solutions to the problem at hand.

#6 started off with, "My name is Jorge Ortega-Gonzales. I have been on the island for over 20 days and have worked hard to make sure that it is safe, and my gang and I will ensure all of your safety." He went on to say, "My gang has checked the island out and found no sign of any other civilization or signs of any other remnants of the society we all came from."

He had a group of 13 individuals that had been working together to make sure the area around us was safe, and they formed an intimidating gang. Jorge was an imposing figure, and he was really good at the art of persuasion and intimidation. Although he never came out and said it, his tone and the use of the word gang had a certain threatening content that you could see was felt by most of the people that had come at the sound of the conch.

As Jorge continued to speak, a general unease fell over the group. One individual asked, "What will our role be?"

Jorge quickly stepped off the platform he had created and, walked over to the individual and, without warning, kicked him in the groin and knocked him violently to the ground.

Members of his gang then went over and carried the man out of sight and made sure everyone knew that questioning Jorge and his gang was not going to be tolerated. He was there to establish his dominance and make sure everyone saw how tough he was and how he had organized a posse that was not to be messed with.

Fear and intimidation seemed to be working, and I had done a good job of staying quiet, hoping other good people would step up and see this for what it was. Unfortunately, with everything else going on, not knowing where we were, why we were here, or what the hell was going on, that didn't happen.

I had said earlier that I was going to sit back and listen, find out what was going on, and not get involved; well, I guess the old coach in me came out.

I walked out from the back of the crowd and immediately challenged Jorge. I asked, "Who put you in charge?"

Then, I quickly went on to let the other individuals collected on the beach know of the situation I had been involved in the very first night I arrived.

Jorge scoffed, "That's a lie," and started towards me.

I was a little more prepared for him this time. His first move was to get me to react, but I stood my ground and didn't flinch. He came straight at me and went with a flying roundhouse that I ducked away from and gave him a quick jab in the ribs. It probably didn't inflict much pain, but at least I had struck first.

Let me share with you that at this time, you can practice defense and counterattacks all you want, but when it comes right down to it, it's not "real till it's real," and Jorge caught me with a cross that about knocked me out, then followed with a kick to the gut and finished it with another punch to the face. It hurt, but I had decided to do this, and I ducked his next roundhouse and squarely got a haymaker into his jaw and face. It stunned him a little, and I went after him, but again, his ultimate fighting experience took over, and he tackled me and beat the shit out of me.

I didn't have any water to protect me this time, and as he continued to pummel me, I didn't have too much resistance to offer, but I wouldn't quit. He knocked me down two more times, and I got in one or two more successful hits, but it was going nowhere fast.

Finally, Don and, Jessie, and a couple of people stepped out of the crowd to intervene. Most of the crowd was even more confused with this whole thing, but they stepped up and came to my rescue. It was stupid, but I wasn't going to let a bully come in and influence and intimidate people who already were confused and disoriented. I felt I had to do something to change the tone that Jorge was trying to set, and if it meant getting the crap kicked out of me, then that was what I had to do.

I wasn't sure what was going on in this new world, but I'd be damned if I was going to sit by and let some egotistical jerk make choices before we had a chance to make informed decisions about the future of all the people that had been "planted" here, for whatever reason. I'd taught history and knew enough about dictators and fascists to know that fear and intimidation were not the best ways to start a new world if that, in fact, was what we were doing, and I was willing to get my ass kicked to get good people to stand up and not allow that to happen.

Thankfully, I think that is what happened. I wasn't sure because I'm pretty sure I lost consciousness and woke up a day later in some type of makeshift hospital room. I had accomplished being the first person on the island to get beat up and have the need for some type of emergency treatment; it had been a great start to the week.

As I came out of the stupor caused by a concussion, I started to see a familiar sight. Kim, the nurse I had met on my explorations, was constantly at my side. She was great, offering me water and some liquids to help me gain back my strength.

She couldn't help but tell me, "That was one of the stupidest things she had ever seen." Jorge was a big, strong guy, and I was no match for him, and "I could have gotten killed." She went on to tell me that after the fight, "Jorge had left, and the crowd supported me and what I had said,"

Kim was the positive young lady that I thought she would be when we first met, and I appreciated her warmth and genuine kindness the next few days. I also met the doctor and a key player in saving me from Jorge. I quickly came to know Dr. Linn, #9, the doctor who was treating my injuries. He was constantly checking my vitals and making sure I wasn't going to be the first person on the island to die.

After a few days, I met another individual that I found out later was instrumental in me not getting pummeled even more at the beach with Jorge. Michael, #1, was a navy seal and had stepped up when Jorge had continued to rock my world. He, Don, Jessie, and some other guys had stopped the beating and helped to disperse the crowd and get some semblance of order back after the chaos of the first "town meeting" on our new island.

The next few days were a fog, but Kim and some other people helping told me, "Jorge and his gang left the beach, and no one had heard from them since."

Michael continued, "Most of the people on the beach respected what you did and appreciated you getting pummeled to make a point." He also pointed out, "No one else was willing to stand up to Jorge, and I talked to a lot of people that wish they would have reacted sooner."

There was a lot of apprehension about what was going to happen next, but a group had assembled after the beach incident and talked about trying to form some type of counsel to start to answer some questions and see if there was any consensus on the next steps we should take. They were going to wait until I was a little healthier because of the respect I had gained for being willing to take on the gang and suffer the consequences of that decision.

I felt somewhat honored, but it didn't help the real pain I was feeling from getting hammered again by Jorge. This guy was not good for the island, and I realized there was little I could do to stop the impact he could have. I wasn't a violent person, but I couldn't help thinking that if he were dead, it wouldn't hurt my feelings. I just wasn't sure I could do it, even if I had to. I just didn't have it in me.

When I worked with at-risk students, I always believed there weren't bad kids, just kids who made bad decisions. I was hoping Jorge was an individual who was making bad choices, but I can't lie. Over my career, I have encountered a few kids who were bad seeds, and they were troubled in every sense of the word. I'd have to try to figure out which kid Jorge was.

Over the next few days, Dr. Linn stopped by and started to discuss how I was doing and the next steps to a full recovery. He had noticed, "I was healing rapidly, faster than normal."

I had already started to feel a lot better, and the bruises and internal injuries Dr. Linn felt were "coming along nicely."

We discussed that not many people had had the injuries I had, and they didn't have much information other than a couple of minor abrasions, but everyone they had dealt with seemed to have healed more quickly than normal. I was sort of their case study on the healing powers that seemed to exist on the island. One more mystery in this new world. In my case, I was glad because it sucked getting beat up in the first place, twice, but at least I healed quickly. I wondered if anyone had checked on Jorge. I had got one or two decent hits in, and I wondered if he had the same recuperative powers or if I was just special.

Michael, the navy seal, also liked to come in and visit. I think it was to see Kim more than me, but I found he and the doctor had become good friends, and he was interested in my story. When we talked, he told me, "I was either the dumbest man he had ever meant or the bravest," coming from a navy seal, that was quite a compliment, I thought, I mean the brave part.

He also told me my fighting techniques "left a lot to be desired" and "he could teach me some things that might help me if I were ever in that situation again."

He respected what I had done and thought some training might be a good idea, not just for me but for anyone who might want to be prepared for those types of interactions. We were starting to realize that this new place might not be a utopia, and we might have to have plans to defend ourselves from each other. That was a scary thought. From most of my original encounters, most of the people I had come to meet had been good, solid individuals who were hard workers and seemed to have strong basic values concerning right and wrong, but I also realized that it took time to get to know someone and that as we continued to navigate this new land, time was something we might have plenty of.

Chapter Seven: #6 = Jorge Ortega-Gonzales

#6 name is Jorge Ortega-Gonzales. Jorge was a successful "businessman" in the difficult drug trade. He worked his way up the system to be one of the major leaders in a gang in Denver. He started as a runner, and through hard work, using his brain to navigate a difficult life and community and understanding the individuals around him, Jorge worked to be a successful part of his community. He was taught early how to live on the streets and do what was necessary to stay alive and out of jail. He understood the importance of knowing the people around him, who he could trust, and who he had to be one step ahead of.

Jorge was ruthless when he needed to be and compassionate when necessary. He had a loyal group of friends who helped him to do the things he needed to be successful in his trade. Yet he also realized that he had to be careful and was not above using intimidation and fear to accomplish his goals.

He also worked to become one of the best ultimate fighters in the world and has quite a reputation for annihilating his competition in the ring. Jorge was a muscular, 6'2" Latino who had worked hard on his physical appearance and skills. He was tough and resilient and had worked hard to be successful in his position.

This new island is causing Jorge a lot of anxiety. He comes from a world where he knows who he can trust and has a close circle of friends. He couldn't open up to new people because of the risk that was involved with people outside his circle. His fighting prowess and skills give him a valuable skill set in any circumstance, and he is confident in most settings. This new environment will be a whole new game to navigate and figure out what to do to gain the status he had in Denver.

Jorge is still trying to figure out what is going on. He gets up every morning and doesn't get it: Where am I? How did I get here? He has never been around water, and when he was young, he saw the film "Jaws" and ever since has had a phobia about getting in the water. He has never lived around water and has never shared this with any of his friends, and he does everything he can to avoid being around bodies of water.

Jorge is struggling with his first encounter in this new place. When he first arrived, he saw a young lady and was trying to ask her what was going on when she freaked out and started screaming. He hadn't meant any harm, but she must have seen a Latino and just went crazy. Then the other guy appeared, #98. and he had been so frustrated with the girl that he took it out on the guy. It was just a reflex; he kind of felt bad, but the other guy deserved it, getting into his business like that.

Jorge has been prowling the beach, looking for other individuals to see if he can find anyone who knows him or some of his gang. He is careful and quickly makes contact with three other individuals who have been "planted" on the island. These three individuals all have similar clothing and have numbers #27, #38, and #64. #27 was a businessman in Chicago. He had been successful, lived in a nice area in the Gold Coast area, and built a solid business in the tech field. #38 had been in the communications industry. He had worked for the cable company, had worked his way up the ladder and knew his way around the internet, and was on his way to being an influencer of some type. He just wasn't sure what he was going to influence. #64 was a bartender on the beach in Florida. He got all the right shifts, knew how to treat customers, and was friendly to everyone he met. He could make a mean Margarita and was good with the ladies. He had lived in Florida all his life, and the terrain they were in seemed like home to him. He understood the weather and the conditions and used that to help navigate the new surroundings.

When they met Jorge, they all connected in a business sense, and they agreed to stay together and use each other's skills to make the best of everything until they could figure it out. They had a lot of conversations about what was going on? Where they are? and How do they get out of here and back to their homes? All have different skill sets and have come from a variety of backgrounds but can't come up with any plausible explanations and have started to settle into a routine here.

They are continuing to adapt and find ways to make it in this new place that they really don't understand. They have added nine more people to their camp in the forest and continue to try to find a way off the "island" or at least survive and prosper until they figure things out.

Chapter Eight: Next steps

After the meeting, different groups of individuals tried to follow up on some issues we were all facing. The first issue that some individuals started to grapple with was how long we had been on the island. The best guess was that most had been "planted" about 4-5 weeks ago, and we were into approximately our 30th day, about a month. There was a lot of chatter about having some way to keep track of the days, weeks, and months in the future.

Soni, #71, a master gardener, had a solid understanding of the seasons and said, "I can try to look at the crops and plant life and, based on the information I uncover, can start to try to develop some type of calendar to guide us."

She continued, "I'll do my best to develop the calendar around the plants indigenous to the island so we can start to try to figure out what the days, weeks, and months have in common with where we came from."

Ivan Zawosky, #77, a horticulturist, offered his assistance and said, "By working with Soni and tracking some of the plants we have identified, we may be able to figure out the various seasons and plan out when the best time to plant would be."

The two oversaw looking into this and coming up with a reasonable calendar and when the best time to plant would be and then use it as a guide for our time on this island. That way, we could start using days of the week to plan upcoming events, start charting the different seasons, and look at if there were certain times it would be better to plant certain crops and keep a history of what was going to take place in the future.

Another group that was on the island would start to get a count and identify the different people that were populating the island. Katie, #45, an accountant, and Hamir, #46, a statistician for the census bureau, started to get a list of all the people they had come into contact with the last few weeks.

Since the fiasco on the beach, more people were meeting informally and bringing in items to share and barter for. This would give Katie and Hamir a chance to identify all the people's names they could find, record their number, what they had done in the previous world, and what attributes they had that could help in the development of our new society.

We were organizing a calendar, finding out who was part of our world, and a real farmers market was developing that provided a variety of products. It gave people a chance to talk and have conversations about what they were feeling and possible ways to work together until someone figured out what was going on.

Other than the uncertainty of Jorge and his gang, a mini-society was starting to develop, and supply and demand were starting to impact the choices of the environment everyone was a part of. A true community was forming, and people were starting to feel more comfortable in this new place, and people were starting to discuss things that had been on everyone's mind since they got here. Where is here? Why are we here? How did we get here? How long are we here for? Will we ever see our loved ones again? What's with the numbers?

After a few days, Dr. Linn, Michael, Kim, and some others decided to start a discussion night and, based on Soni and Ivan's calendar, would meet every Tuesday evening. Everyone was invited, and they would tackle one of the questions that was on everyone's mind.

By this time, it had been established that counting Jorge's band of 13, there were 91 people accounted for. #19, #37, #49, #51, #66, #72, #73, #84 and #100 were unaccounted for. Everyone else between 1-100 had been accounted for, and it was generally accepted this new world had or was supposed to have 100 people.

I joked that "the seniors in my high school had a senior prank where the seniors let four chickens run loose in the school and numbered them #1, #2, #3, and #5. The principals spent most of the day looking for #4. I hoped this wasn't a cruel joke, but was pretty sure those nine people were missing, and we needed to find them.

The final count was 46 males and 45 females, a wide diversity as far as cultural and ethnic backgrounds were concerned. Most had held respectable jobs, and when asked, most felt they were solid, steady, reliable, respected by peers, and overall above average. They wouldn't say they were great, but they were pretty good and felt that they had accomplished most of the things they were trying to.

Pretty much every job you could think of was recorded, from politician to doctor, educator to farmer, hairdresser to computer programmer. Many of these jobs were translating to providing many of the essentials needed to make a productive society, one that could provide the safety and security needs of the people living here.

The youngest person was Kim at 34 and the oldest was myself at 64. Most had a high school education or some type of college degree, and 79 of the individuals had close family ties, whether it be a spouse, significant other, or kids and parents that they were close to and thought about a lot.

The town's first discussion had around 75 people, most everyone other than Jorge's gang and the individuals that were unaccounted for. Everyone was afforded the opportunity to offer their thoughts on why we thought we were chosen to be on this island. Was there any commonality? Did we know similar people? Were we from the same regions? Could there be a common thread that tied us together?

Most had come to the realization that although they didn't know how or why they were chosen to be, 100 people were here, and that was too big a coincidence to just have happened.

The Reverand Pat Findle, #31, a minister from Florida, was the first to offer his thoughts; "God has put us here!" Reverand Findle felt that God had chosen these fine people to be here. We were going to start a new world, and we had the chance to make amends for a world that was out of control. God had decided to have a "do-over," and we were the ones he decided to do it all over with.

Several participants gave Reverand Findle an "amen!"

Michael got up and said, "It has to be the government!" He stated with conviction, "This was a secret, clandestine operation that wanted to see how a group of normal people from every walk of life and every possible culture and ethnic background would develop and communicate with each other and what kind of society would develop." This operation was seeing whether "we would work together? or constantly get into conflict?"

This was all an experiment to see the behavioral patterns of individuals put into an unfamiliar setting to see how they would react. The government had the resources and ability to pull this off. They identified us, drugged us, and secretly transported us to a remote location and were watching everything through secret cameras placed throughout the island.

You could see people in the audience nodding. A couple of individuals got up and brought up aliens and how we could have been transported to this place to see how humans would react in a controlled environment.

The last man to speak was #41, Kiran. He was a computer tech and was really involved in the AI universe. You could tell he was good at his job yet could talk in ways a non-computer literate person would understand. Kiran went on to explain he didn't see the way this could happen but said, "AIs are scary!"

As he continued to program the different AI functions, he often felt, "The AIs were way ahead of us, almost like they were toying with us."

Although it seemed the scientists developing these AIs were in control, he felt the AIs were just letting them think they were in control, but the AIs were manipulating and leading the techs where to go. He wondered out loud, "Did these AIs develop a type of algorithm that had made all of us think we were here and were using this as a way to see how humans would deal with complex situations so they could gain a greater understanding of the humans to be able to better control them in the future."

WOW! That blew me away. I always would tell my wife that we had to be careful about what we said in front of Siri. One time, I was discussing the bus routes around town, and the next day, on Facebook, I received a bus schedule.

I don't want to sound paranoid, but if these supercomputers can process things as fast as they say they can, shouldn't we be worried that they know a lot more and how to fake, not showing what they are capable of?

My running joke was, "I was moving to Casper, Wyoming, going to blow up the cell towers and set up a perimeter where we could see them coming."

I figured their greatest weakness would be a lack of connectivity, and in the middle of Wyoming, it would be the best place to hide out. Everyone in Casper has a gun, a pickup truck, and enough food and ammunition to wait out any AI attack.

After listening to everyone and their theories of why we were here, I sat back and couldn't help but realize it really didn't matter. We were here, and as far as we were concerned, this is the life we have today. No matter how we got here or who put us here, this was our reality. I didn't mind hearing what others had to say, but this is the hand we were dealt; let's play it the best we can and see where it takes us.

I learned a long time ago that you have to control the things you can control. Worrying about why we were here, I couldn't control that, but I could control what we did when we were here. Common sense says we need to figure out what it takes for all to be safe, happy, and productive.

That's what we were looking for in our earlier lives on Earth; now, we just have a different reality, and we need to make the best of it. Whether it is God, the government, aliens, or AIs, it doesn't matter. What matters is making the best of what we have, being resilient, enjoying what we are doing, and helping those around us. It ~~just~~ doesn't matter why; we are here, let's just do our best to support everyone and make it the best world it can be.

I listened, and when everyone was finished, I shared my thoughts. I didn't have answers to the questions on everyone's mind, but I did have pragmatic, common-sense ideas that we could focus on. That's what I wanted to discuss.

After the meeting, it was decided that the Tuesday night discussions would still happen, but the community needed to start planning the next steps. Would we have a ruling group? How would it be chosen? What would it deal with? How would it get input? There were a lot of pragmatic concerns that someone was going to have to figure out, and this community had to decide the process we would follow. We pretty much all agreed that we were here to stay, at least for the near future, and we had better have a plan.

Chapter Nine: Let's PARTY!

The rest of the night, people hung out and talked. It was nice. As the evening progressed, we found out that a number of individuals had unique talents in the area of fun.

A couple of the scientists had been experimenting with homemade alcoholic beverages and had some success in developing a tasty brew that had a decent amount of alcoholic content.

Marijuana had been located by another group and cultivated and was seen as an excellent stress reliever.

Others were closet cooks and had developed some fun recipes they wanted to share.

It was decided that Friday night, we should have a shindig on the beach. We would spread the word and have a social gathering with everyone pitching in to make sure all the needs were provided for. Food, refreshments, and all the fixins.

It hopefully would end up being an interesting night, and everyone could look forward to meeting Maslow's love and belonging needs. I couldn't wait to meet new individuals and have a social conversation with people I might be spending the rest of my life with, and I have to admit, good food, good company, and a beer couldn't hurt reduce the anxiety and apprehensions we all had about the situation we continued to find ourselves in.

The rest of the week, there was a buzz, and people were constantly down on the beach, planning and getting ready for the party that had been planned. It was fascinating to watch the creative ways people came up with to make sure the party was a success, from making bamboo cups and plates to figuring out what type of fun things could be planned to have some fun and have genuine conversations with other people they had seen on the island.

A group of people wondered whether we should invite Jorge, but we decided maybe the next time we could. There was too much bad blood between the two groups, and sometime in the future we should see whether we could fix things and if they wanted things to be fixed, but now wasn't the right time.

Friday night came along, and the beach was packed. People brought homemade chairs to sit on and games like Jenga and Cornhole to play that they had made during the week. There was plenty of food and beverages, and it was a real party. It was a great way to take some pressure out of our everyday lives and just build relationships and talk to people. I saw Dr. Linn and Michael; they were talking with Kim and Tanver.

Katie and Hamir were pointing at people, and I know they wished they could have had a way to make nametags so they could check all the work they had put into tracking who was on the island. A few people even made homemade clothes so they wouldn't have to wear their T-shirt with a number on it.

The party really started when Don, Jessie, and Louis arrived. They'd evidently met Jessica Morgan, Kathy, and a couple of other young ladies and were having a lot of fun. They'd made some moonshine and must have had a pre-party bash before coming. It sort of reminded me of Friday night socials where the whole town got together and had some fun. People were talking and getting to know each other, and alcohol was a new addition to the new world and was having the necessary effect.

Parties are nice, but I'm not really good at small talk, so I just listened and watched people. It was fascinating seeing the different groups interact. As I listened, I realized the numbers people were assigned was a big topic of discussion. I heard one group say, "You must be special if you are in the top 10."

Another countered with, what if you are in the bottom 10? Does that mean you can't do anything?"

I took a little offense at that; I was #98. Most people wondered how you got the number you got and what they must mean.

The other topic I heard continually was about how much they missed their families back home. You could see that although most were resigned to being here, they missed the people in their lives who had been a major part of their world, and now they had no clue if they'd ever see them again.

Me, having taught high school psychology and always working with high school students in a social setting, it was fascinating to see the different ways people interacted and communicated. I'd always been amazed at how students found like-minded kids and became friends or, in some cases, enemies. How those relationships had developed or exploded, and how, in some cases, some students even knew each other. They had come from such different backgrounds. I enjoyed watching the different individuals socialize and then try to see what their background was. It was a true social experiment in every way, and I couldn't help but feel that we were all part of a big case study on human behavior.

As I was watching the "action," an attractive female that I had never seen came up and asked me, "What are you doing?"

I wasn't being totally aloof, but I had not mingled very much, other than saying "hi" to the individuals I knew, having a conversation about my health with Dr. Linn, Katie, and Michael, and having some fun trading insults with Don, Jessie, and Louis. She sort of caught me just lost in my thoughts and told me she had been intrigued by the curious look on my face as I watched the events of the evening unfold.

I explained, "I love watching people and trying to figure out the social and emotional behaviors of students for over 40 years." I continued, "It's fascinating to just watch people and try to figure out why they were the way they were."

I'd always learned to try to see the positives in the kids in my school, and it was exciting to see that so many good people had been "planted" on this island. I was looking forward to meeting them and getting to know them. I then introduced myself and asked her name.

"I'm Paige," she exclaimed quietly yet confidently.

I could already see she was #2. That in itself was impressive, and a little intimidating, although I wasn't sure why.

She went on to explain, "I'm a clinical psychiatrist at John Hopkins and am interested in a lot of the same things."

I really felt stupid talking about social-emotional development when I found out she had her doctorate in the field, and I must have looked kind of sheepish because she made it clear she "appreciated my take on high school student behavior and the comparison to the situation we were in now."

She immediately made me feel at ease and talked about the different worlds she and I came from when it came to understanding the people around us. She explained, "She dealt mainly with troubled adults and was constantly trying to figure out what made people do the things they did and the justifications they used to make them seem normal."

For the next hour, we just talked about things we knew about and got lost in the conversation. The more we talked, the more I realized we had a lot in common, but at the same time, we had come from completely different backgrounds. She had strong opinions on a variety of subjects, from our current president to her thoughts on our public education system. She had grown up in the city and had never been on a farm. We found out that although we disagreed on a lot of things and came from different backgrounds, we had fun and found we could talk about a lot of things we couldn't talk to our friends and family about.

We were having a pretty intense discussion when, all of a sudden, Don and Jessie decided we were being anti-social. They'd had a good bit to drink and decided to lighten up the mood by throwing bamboo buckets of water on us and making sure everyone at the party saw them do it. Alcohol was having the same impact in the new world as it had in the old. People who needed to relieve some stress got drunk and could forget all that was going on around them and act like total idiots.

After Paige and I dried off, we went out amongst the rest of the islanders and introduced each other to the people in our circles whom we had met the past week. Paige's best friend was an engineer named Ariana Rachowski, #10, and a Dietician named Selina Hernandez-Ramirez, #14. Colby Miller, #16, an FBI agent, was an acquaintance, and after spending the rest of the evening with these guys, along with Kim, Michael, and Dr. Linn, I determined that the individuals I had encountered could develop into a strong team, a team that could deal with all the challenges this new land could present.

Karaoke started, and as it progressed, we all realized there were some talented people in our midst. A young lady, #68, C.J. Jones, sang and had everyone mesmerized with her Linda Ronstadt songs. Then, a trio of individuals sang some Zach Brown songs, and the place went wild. People were dancing and having a great time.

Just when there were all these feelings of positivity, all hell broke loose. People started taking their clothes off and skinny dipping. Some people were upset and started yelling at them. Others got involved by making inappropriate comments about some of the rowdy ones. They brought up that they should have expected that from people with numbers above 50 and that "those" types of people were going to hurt our chances of survival.

Luckily, the sober individuals were able to bring some type of order to the evening, but a few things had been said and heard, and we saw a little of "The Lord of the Flies" sneak into our new world. Assumptions were made about why individuals had the numbers they did, and I was surprised to hear those judgments, but after remembering some of the things I had heard Tuesday when people were just having general discussions, I wasn't totally surprised.

Chapter Ten: #2 = Paige Richards

#2, Paige Richards grew up in Philadelphia, Pennsylvania. She was the youngest in a family of overachievers and never knew exactly what she wanted to do in life until she became part of the Big Sisters of Philadelphia. She connected with a couple of kids at the meetings and enjoyed getting to know and working with them on their schoolwork. She realized she had a pretty cushy life, and if she could find ways to help less fortunate kids, it would be good for her and valuable for her community. Her parents weren't overly enthused with the idea, but Paige could be stubborn, and when her parents didn't like the idea, she liked it even more.

She worked her way through college and grad school and gradually found her way into the field of Behavioral Psychiatry. She had somehow gotten away from working with children and been fascinated with why "messed up" people got that way and if she could do anything about it. She had a number of patients and did some clinical research in the area of how family life impacted dissociative behavior and developed a pretty solid reputation in her field.

Paige was sort of a free spirit. She came from money, but you'd never know it by the clothes she wore or the company she kept. She loved having fun and hanging out with people with similar interests. Paige is a natural beauty, she is 5'8", has long auburn hair, a fit and developed body, and is willing to show it off.

She had never been in a serious relationship and kept telling herself that the right person hadn't come along yet, but at the same time, she liked her freedom and didn't want to be tied down, at least until she was older. A number of suitors had tried, but she wasn't interested, they weren't her type. Her life right now was fun and work. She had a good balance; she cared about her patients and did her best to give them the support they needed, but could forget about them at night and have some fun. She was good at her job, had developed a strong reputation in the Philadelphia area, and was enjoying life.

Then, out of nowhere, she ends up on this island with a big #2 on her shirt. No clue where she was, why she was here, and how she got here. The more she gets acclimated to her surroundings, the more she likes this place. She has been watching people, and her background has given her the opportunity to witness up close and personal strong feelings of anxiety and angst and the way people deal with it. She has been fascinated by how the different people she has encountered have adjusted to this new environment and how some are thriving. Others are struggling with the situation and the coping mechanisms they are using. It is like a gigantic social experiment, and she has a front-row seat to look at human behavior in a controlled situation.

She's not crazy about having the #2; it seems ambiguous, and she is unsure why she has been assigned the number, but those around her seem to give her more status due to the number on her clothing. She's still figuring out the social dynamics of this situation and the numbers various individuals have been assigned.

One guy has intrigued her, #98. He doesn't seem like he should be the #98. He seems bright, articulate and has a pretty good sense of humor. There must be something wrong with him. I mean, he is #98, but he seems like a nice guy, and she has let him flirt with her. She'll take her time and see where this goes, but it is kind of fun, and she considers it part of her case study on individuals' behavior in the new world.

Chapter Eleven: What's up with these #'s and why are some missing?

The next day, everyone talked about the party and all the different things that happened. Some discussed the entertainment, others the wild activities of the individuals who had too much to drink, and others that hooked up after the party and how great it felt to connect with someone.

There was an undercurrent of what happened at the night's end and the conflict over the numbers people had been assigned or were wearing. Something a little weird was circulating; people who had discarded their numbered T-shirts and made their own shirts, when they got up this morning, their number was on the shirt they had made. This was really weird and was freaking a number of individuals out.

As people continued to talk, myself, Dr. Linn, Paige, Kim, Colby, and Michael got together and started talking about everything that was going on, especially the whole number deal. Michael started by talking about his #1. He said, "I'm not sure why I'm #1, and I don't like being "given" this number."

I asked, "How do you think I feel? I'm #98." I asked him, "Do you want to switch?"

Most of the people in this group were in the lower digits, which made for interesting conversation and a little awkward.

Katie and Hamir interrupted the discussion and started reviewing the list of people we had encountered. We knew that approximately 8-10 people were missing, and Colby, the FBI agent, wondered, "Where are these people, and are they in any type of danger?"

We weren't sure how many people were a part of Jorge's gang, but we needed to know and try to track down the individuals still not identified. I didn't know Colby very well, but I could tell he was concerned about the missing people, and when we started to press, he said he "Just felt that something didn't seem right. Why wouldn't people come to the beach?"

A couple of attempts had been made with the conch, and no one had seen these people in all the weeks leading up to today. He didn't want to panic but believed we needed to work hard on figuring out whether these individuals were now part of Jorge's gang or were they somewhere out in the forest and possibly needed help.

We determined we would do two things in the next few days. First, we would develop a search party that would do a day-by-day search of the areas we knew existed on the island. Don, Jessie, Louis, and Brodie would head up a team and do an extensive search of the island. They all had experience in hunting and knew their way around rough terrain.

There was also a group of runners that had mapped out the island led by two females who had been active triathletes, Kerri Washington, #60, and Hayley Thompson, #29, who offered to share all their information and where they had been. After discussing all the information, they explained, "There are only a few places they knew of that no one had been, and we should probably concentrate the search in these areas. It was rough terrain, and there was a chance someone could have fallen or been injured without anyone knowing."

Another group would make a peaceful journey to Jorge's camp and get a count of individuals who were part of his gang. It was estimated that there were about 15-20, but it was unclear what numbers they wore and whether were they part of his gang by choice. It would be a touchy undertaking, and whoever went needed to understand that there was a possibility of conflict.

It was determined Dr. Linn, Michael, Colby, Paige, Kim, Valerie Chen, #12, a lawyer out of Los Angeles, Katie, our accountant and numbers person, and I would go.

Michael, Valerie Chen, and Dr. Linn asked me, "Do you think you should go?'

There was a lot of discussion about how Jorge would respond to me because of the history Jorge had.

I responded, "I needed to figure out if we could co-exist on the same island," and "I would like to go and see where things went."

A lot of females had been chosen, so it would seem we were not looking for conflict. We all hoped with Valerie there to negotiate and Kim and Dr. Linn to address any medical concerns, we could avoid conflict, get our numbers, and even possibly develop lines of communication for the future. This could be an advantageous trip.

Chapter Twelve: Earning respect

At sunrise the next morning, the search parties and the team going to Jorge's camp headed out to try to solve the mystery of the missing #'s and see if we could start to mend relationships with the group that had fractioned after the first town meeting.

We knew where Jorge's group was located and, after hiking to their camp, loudly introduced why we had come and what we needed. Jorge and his second in command, Deryl Walker, #21, a welder from Syracuse, New York, met us at the entrance to their camp. Dr. Linn and Colby did most of the talking and explained the purpose of our visit.

They explained, "We are just trying to see how your group is doing and if there is anything we can do to help."

Jorge listened and, after consulting with Deryl, asked us to come into the camp where we could all talk. I'm not saying it was a warm welcome. I got the feeling we were walking into an interesting situation; some might call it a trap. Once inside their camp, we saw a nice setup. They had several huts that people evidently lived in, a smoke shack to smoke their fish and chickens or ducks they had caught. There was one area set up with various fruits and vegetables that had been collected, and there was a definite feeling of safety in the camp.

Once inside, Katie started gathering information, and Dr. Linn and Kim asked if anyone needed any medical attention. There were some minor abrasions and cuts, and it did seem as if most of the individuals had some type of bruises from fighting and some type of altercations.

When Kim and Dr. Linn questioned the group, Jorge spoke up and said, "Once a week, we have a "competition" to hone our fighting skills, and it was intense and led to some injuries, but nothing major." He said, "There is a competition tonight, and if we stayed, maybe we could be a part of the competition." He looked directly at Michael, Colby, and myself as he spoke.

Tonight's activity would be for the males in the group. Next week both females and males would be part of the competition. It was an intriguing idea, but I wasn't sure I wanted to get my ass kicked again, and I wasn't sure how Michael and Colby felt about the idea.

When we hesitated, Jorge was clear that he didn't believe we could hack the competition, and there was no need to feel we "had" to participate. It was his way of challenging us in front of his gang and the other individuals with us that he and his gang were superior and others were welcome to be a part of his gang if they could "take" it.

Jorge said, "The rules are simple; there aren't any. You will be put in with another competitor for three minutes and simply hone your fighting skills."

Winners were determined by the number of blows that each fighter registered, and each member of his gang had a rating based on their success/failure in the competition. You could be in as many as three fights per competition, and at the end of the day, all competitors partied together. I guess we weren't the only people on the island that had figured out ways to have fun if that's what you call getting your ass kicked.

Michael, a Navy seal, and Colby, an FBI agent, took the bait, automatically said they were in and looked forward to the competition. Of course, they both had training and were very experienced in this type of stuff.

The focus then shifted to me. Everyone was staring. I hadn't covered myself with glory in my last two "fights," although I had been training with Michael, I still wasn't anywhere close to where I needed to be, but "What the Hell!" I also said I would enter the competition.

It was around 3 o'clock. The competition would start in two hours. We would have a chance to finish up our count and then have a little time to prepare with our team. In that hour, everyone started talking about our decision, the females were mad because we had to be so macho. We could get our information and get out, but the males realized this was a chance to build relationships through respect. If we just walked away, Jorge and his gang would feel we were pussies, and they would have an edge if we ever did get into a conflict. If we could compete, it could go a long way in helping us work with this group in the future.

As we got closer to the competition, I got a little more apprehensive. Jorge's gang had evidently been practicing and were probably pretty good at this type of fighting. I had been practicing with Michael but still was not what I would call proficient in ultimate fighting.

When the competition started, I saw I was paired in three rounds. I didn't have to fight Jorge, but I did see I was pitted against Deryl, Jorge's second in command.

Michael was first. Remember, he was a navy seal, 6'1", and built like a rock. It was no contest; Michael landed more blows than his opponent and even knocked him to the ground on several occasions.

Colby was next, an FBI agent and, again, solid and with a lot of experience. Again, no contest, Colby defeated his man easily and showed a lot of experience in the situation.

After watching the prowess of the fighters Michael and Colby had shown, I figured I might have a shot.

Wrong, Deryl was strong, knowledgeable, and ready to kick my ass. He came at me aggressively, and although I blocked and deflected a number of his advances, I took enough hits to know I'd been in a fight. He won, and although I had defended myself well, I had enough bruises to feel defeated.

Two more rounds with similar results. It seemed like each round, the competition for Colby and Micheal stayed consistent. In my case, I seemed to get the crème of the crop. Michael and Colby won all three of their fights, and I ended up 0-3. The best thing I could say was I didn't have any broken ribs and just a couple of bruises on my face.

After the competition, we all "bonded" by sitting around and drinking some alcohol. It did seem Jorge and his gang would leave the main party and do "something." I'm not sure if they had some harder drugs and were partaking away from us, but both Colby and I noticed a definite glaze and different "attitude" when they returned. Colby had dealt with enough individuals who had been strung out on drugs and committed crimes that he could see certain behaviors in the group we were with. In my case, I had dealt with enough high, dazed students under the influence that the behavior I was witnessing showed many of the same characteristics.

The affair was interesting, and you could tell that Jorge and his gang were trying to recruit some of the members of our party to come back maybe and be a part of theirs. Paige and Kim were definite targets, and Jorge and Deryl were aggressively pursuing them, but I thought they were entrenched with us. Valerie Chen, the lawyer, seemed to be the most influenced, and you could see she was intrigued by the "action" she had witnessed throughout the evening.

The rest of the evening was relatively uneventful; there were no fights, and the issue of numbers never came up in Jorge's camp. It seemed more like a chess game than a party, and each side was figuring out their next moves as the evening progressed. I got the feeling that although we got information about who was part of Jorge's gang, they were trying to get information about our group and how they could get people in our group to join theirs. I also realized that Jorge was an intelligent individual who could fight and be a threat or ally, depending on how it all played out.

I also saw a side of some of Jorge's gang members that were aggressive and possibly violent if they didn't get their way. All the individuals that I fought with wanted to hurt me, and when I continued to defend myself, they became more and more aggressive and frustrated. I got the feeling that Jorge had wanted to make me look bad again, and when they didn't beat the crap out of me, he was disappointed. That evening, I honestly believed that if I were alone, they would have jumped me and inflicted as much bodily harm as they could have, so I was careful to stay with my friends all night.

When we got up in the morning, we all reviewed what we had found out about who was part of Jorge's gang that we were unaware of. We found there were six total, three females and three males. They were #19, Dave Valesky, a police officer from New York. Anthony Vacarro, #66, an upstanding citizen who "maybe" had ties to the mob in Atlantic City, and Sam Watkins, #84, a rather entrepreneurial homeless man from Portland, Oregon.

All seemed loyal to Jorge and had bought into the ultimate fighting lifestyle and whatever else was going on in his camp. I don't want to sound prejudicial, but these individuals seemed to be a fit for the lifestyle Jorge was offering, had a mean streak, were acclimating to the new environment, and liked the freedom Jorge's camp offered them.

The females were different. Marcie Skrinjar, #72, and Nancy Schmid, #73, were in the field of education. They seemed to be solid citizens and had come from family backgrounds that didn't mesh with Jorge's gang. I think there might have been some fear, and the two had been caught up in this group and never really had an opportunity to get out, and now, knowing there were other possibilities on the island, might leave if the chance presented itself.

The last female, Cheryl Thiel, #37, was beautiful, had a great body, and had been a model. She seemed self-absorbed and dangerous. I couldn't put my finger on it, but she scared me. She was nice, but I had been around enough individuals with dark sides, and something about Cheryl told me she was not someone you wanted to get on her bad side. It seemed she and Jorge were an item, and the two of them together created a powerful couple that could intimidate and control those around them.

Jorge's camp was everything that the camp we were forming wasn't. There was definitely a component of danger and foreboding. I couldn't say for sure, but the group seemed to be developing harder drugs that impacted behavior more, and that was a part of the old-world culture that I would rather not see introduced here. I had dealt with too many individuals who didn't need that type of false support here because it had become a crutch for them in the world we came from and impacted their ability to function and be productive. We had identified 19 members of Jorge's gang and overall felt that the trip had been productive as far as finding out the number of people on the island.

When we were together the night before, we all wondered whether they would let us leave in the morning, but no problems arose. On the way home, my group, especially Colby and Michael, were on me about not winning any battles. The girls sort of chimed in, and I was getting a lot of grief.   After about 20 minutes, I asked, "How do I look?"

They thought it was a weird question, and everyone stopped, and Michael asked, "Why is that important?"

I asked, "Do I have a lot of bruises?"

They answered, "No."

I asked, "On a scale of 1-10, how do I look as far as bumps and bruises?"

They all answered, "About a 5-6."

I then went on to explain that although I didn't win any competitions, I learned a lot. All three individuals that I fought gave me their best shot. I learned "What they had and how to defend it." I continued to explain, "I wasn't in the competition to win; I was in it to find out about Jorge's gang and what we needed to be aware of. If we met them again, I learned some valuable information that I could possibly use in the future."

I also explained, "Those guys think I'm a puss and are pretty sure I was the weak link. If they needed to take one of us out, it would be me."

I proceeded to explain that I liked being underestimated. I had worked in a predominantly Latino school, and the kids felt I was "just a dumb old white guy."

I was OK with that because the dumber they thought I was, the more they would tell me. I learned that by getting people to underestimate you and not feel you were a threat went a lot further than trying to prove how tough you were.

I then asked Michael and Colby if they had "shown" their best stuff, and they said, "Yes," they wanted to prove to Jorge that they were a threat and they shouldn't be messed with.

I then asked them, "Do you think Jorge's gang learned anything by fighting you? Do you think they learned about your skills and fighting level?"

They answered, "Yes."

I let them think about that and started heading to camp.

Michael yelled up to me, "How are you #98?"

After he listened to my rationale, I think he "got it" and realized he had underestimated me and was thinking about my number and why it was so low. I thought the statement was a little prejudicial but didn't go there. I also hope I have just proven that I was always trying to figure out the next steps, and sometimes, there was more than one way to do that. Hopefully, they would see that the number on my shirt didn't define me and that you were a valuable part of this team no matter what number you wore.

When we got back to camp, the search party was waiting for us, and the news they had for us was disturbing.

Chapter Thirteen: #1 =
Michael Washington

#1 was Michael Washington. Michael was an African American who had moved to the top of his class in the military. He had been highly recruited to become part of the Navy Seals and, once assigned, had been one of their best members. He had taken part in a large number of engagements and was a person the others in his squadron knew would have their back.

He was single, 6"2" and intense. His friends were few, and he trusted only a few close personal acquaintances. A Seal didn't have a girlfriend or wife, although Michael could have his pick. He just never worried about a relationship with a member of the opposite sex, and frankly, he didn't have the time. That was the nature of being a Seal. You knew the job and the territory that went along with it. It consumed your time and thoughts, and you didn't have time for anything else.

Michael had seen a lot during his time as a Seal, and he had done some things he wasn't proud of but understood that these were done for national security and had learned long ago not to ask questions. He had prepared for everything the military could think of and felt he was flexible and resilient enough to handle any situation that might come along.

This was something he hadn't prepared for; to wake up one morning and be on a tropical island with no idea of how he got here, where he was, and who had put him here. He just woke up one morning in a pair of gray shorts and a white shirt with the #1 on it. He immediately thought it was part of his training and, for the first three days, had done reconnaissance on the location and looked for hostiles. During this time, he had seen a variety of individuals who looked dazed and confused and had kept mental notes on the types of individuals he might be dealing with.

None of it made sense. The more he gathered intel, the more confused he got. When he finally made contact with Dr. Linn, a medical doctor, and they compared notes, nothing made sense. No one knew where they were, and feels that he was training for something. He is just not sure what.

Michael had spent over 20 years in the military, and nothing had prepared him for the situation he was now in. He was really struggling with this reality and the role he might play. He had been a Navy Seal; his whole life had been regimented, and his superiors had determined where he would be and when he would be there. In this new world, he had no superiors, and he was in control of everything, although he wasn't sure what that meant.

He had been lucky to meet Dr. Linn and a cute, outgoing nurse named Kim and had developed strong relationships with both. Now, with the whole Conch thing, more people were coming out, and he was like the guy they went to, not because they knew he was a Navy Seal, but because he had the #1 on his shirt, and evidently that meant something, although he wasn't sure what. They were all treating him like the leader, and he wasn't sure he wanted that responsibility. He had been a team leader and seen some things that he still struggled with; he wasn't sure he wanted those responsibilities in a world he didn't understand with people he didn't know.

PHASE II

Chapter Fourteen: A mystery

Brodie spoke for the search team. Between his group and the group that ran and mapped out the island, they had covered pretty much all the island that could be navigated. "There were a lot of mountainous regions that had some treacherous areas."

He explained, "As we were searching, we found a body at the bottom of one of the ravines. Upon further investigation, we found the body of a female with the #100 on her t-shirt."

Nothing else stood out, but all the search team couldn't help but wonder who she was and how confused she must have been. If she had been "planted" in that area and was inexperienced in navigating the outdoors, she easily could have been disoriented and slipped and fallen off the cliff.

Brodie and the other scouts talked and believed "the circumstances were questionable, and they weren't sure if she had died accidentally or not."

Everyone on the search team couldn't help but identify with her and feel terrible about the circumstances.

Both Kerri and Hayley were really upset and wished they knew something else about #100. They wanted to help her, but Brodie and the others felt they needed to leave the scene as clean as they could, and hopefully, someone could put the pieces together and see what they could find out about #100's death. Her body was mangled and decomposed but otherwise intact.

Brodie did explain, "There was some evidence to suggest there could have been someone else in that area at some time."

He had noticed other footprints but was not positive. He didn't have any investigative background and couldn't say for sure the tracks were human or belonged to something else, but he was sure someone or something else had been in that vicinity.

Then, it got even more interesting: they had stumbled across a body in a remote area. From what they could tell, the person, #49, a male, had his neck broken. Again, Brodie wasn't an investigator, but it looked like "The person's body was lying one way, and his head was facing the other direction."

Don and Jessie had stumbled across it first and made sure that no one else but Brodie saw the body, but it had even made Don, Jessie, and Brodie a little squeamish at the sight.

They had identified similar footprints in the area and had marked the spot so others could go back and investigate further. They were all pretty sure that the spot where they found the body was remote enough that very few people, if any, would have been out that far. There was no doubt that this person had been in an altercation and had received the worst end of the deal.

As we listened to the report, Dr. Linn and Colby decided, "We need to see the areas and the bodies."

The search team had left everything pretty much the way they had found it and figured it would need further investigation.

The search team came to one last conclusion. They had travelled the entire island and found no evidence of anyone else out there. That left one individual, #51, unaccounted for. This was puzzling and left everyone wondering where this individual might be hiding or if another body was out there somewhere?

It was decided that the next night we would have a town meeting to inform the rest of the people on the island of what we had found. We also determined Val and Michael would go to Jorge's group and invite them, or a representative of their group, to get the information as well. The last couple of days had been long, hard days, and we needed to keep the rest of the island up to date and get their input on the next steps that needed to be taken.

Chapter Fifteen: Sorting things out

The group I had aligned with, up to this point, was worried about identifying who was and who wasn't there. Another group led by the honorable Ben Hix from the great state of Florida had been trying to decide how this new world was going to be governed.

It made sense, Representative Hix was a politician, and that was his area of expertise. He, along with the Real Estate agent, Bob, and a couple of other civic-minded individuals, had been meeting informally to try to come up with a system of government.

They had tossed a number of ideas around, and when we came around to discuss the next steps, they wondered out loud if we should also "plant some seeds" concerning how we would move forward as a community.

That night, a group of about 12 individuals started to outline how the meeting would go the next night. Words like "community," and "civic responsibility' were thrown around. Most agreed to develop an agenda that would inform and gather input from the community.

There were only 78 people, so it was agreed all should have a say if they wanted to. Representative Hix, Dr. Linn, Paige, and Michael would present various pieces, and we would have an organized discussion on the things listed below.

Representative Hix and Dr. Linn because of their various standing; Doctor and politician, and Michael and Paige because of their #'s. I liked Michael and Paige and respected their knowledge of the situation, but had some reservations about how they should lead us just because of the number they had been assigned. We had no rationale for these assigned #s, and to validate them by allowing #1 and #2 to speak concerned me a little, but I didn't want to be "that guy," and no one else brought it up. The next night, we would present the agenda below.

We would go over the following agenda:

Review the past two months:

1. Reflect on the way we got here.
2. How little we knew about why we were here
3. The dispute with Jorge's community
4. The census we had conducted, 78 = community, 19 = Gang, 3 = ???
5. Our resiliency as far as Safety, Security, Food, and building a community/economy of sorts.
    a. Finding fresh water, fish, and fowl (chickens, ducks, pheasants) to sustain our basic needs

    b. Finding fresh fruits and vegetables to sustain our basic needs.

    c. Developing a system to ensure all the community had resources available to them.

6. Discuss what we found out about the island from the recent exploration team!

    a. We had checked out the whole island and had found no sign of human or animal life.

    b. We had identified that the island was surrounded by water.

    c. The island consisted of lush forests, sandy and rocky beaches, mountains, and rough terrain.

    d. A lot of the island was conducive to living comfortably, but there was some terrain that was unexplored and seemed to be uninhabitable.

Questions we faced.

1. What choices did individuals on the island have?

    a. Did we have to live on the beach in the community that was being developed?

    b. Could we break off and live somewhere else but still use the resources of the community?

    c. Could individuals, if they didn't like the way things were, start their own community?

    d. Could people move in with Jorge's group if they chose to?

2. Discuss how decisions would be made concerning laws and policies that would govern the community.
3. Would we continue to try to find out "what the hell was going on?"

Basically, we were going to try to inform all the people who were part of our community about what we had found, get their input on the next steps because we thought some of them might have been thinking about the same thing, and start to develop a plan for moving forward. Overall, we were just going to try to find out what the people we were living with would like to see in the future. We all realized that there were a lot more questions but decided these were the ones we should tackle first.

We didn't want to bring up the situation with #100, #49 and #51 until we had more information, but that was definitely in the back of a lot of people's minds. Just one more thing to cause stress and anxiety. We also decided to have Val and Colby go to Jorge's gang in the morning and see if they would like to come or send a representative to listen to and be a part of the meeting.

After the meeting, I decided I would see what Paige's thoughts on everything were. As she left, I asked, "Hey, can we talk? I'd like to know your thoughts on your role tomorrow night?" and if there was anything I could do to help her prepare for it.

I thought it was a pretty good way to spend some time with her and I had enjoyed the time we had spent at the party, but over the last few days hadn't had the opportunity to see if she felt the same way.

As I asked, we heard some music coming from the beach. CJ Jones was belting out some Dua Lipa, and it sounded pretty good. We decided to go over and listen, and we figured we could talk about tomorrow night. Hopefully, there will be some alcohol at the beach, and we could have a nice evening.

As we headed over, we saw some others from the meeting with the same idea. Michael and Kim had hooked up, and Bob and Jessica Morgan were heading that way. When we got to the beach, we found it was crowded, and CJ was a big draw.

In fact, I noticed a lot of couples sitting there, taking in the beautiful evening and hanging out. For that night, we all listened to music and forgot that we were on a deserted island and had not been in contact with our family or friends for over two months. We enjoyed the music and the companionship.

CJ finished up, and the couple started to mingle and break up. Paige and I said "Hi" to Michael and Kim,

Bob came over, and we talked for a little with him and Jessica.

Bob shared some ideas on what he thought about our next steps concerning the government and how "we had to let a free market run freely." We talked casually for the next few minutes and

I hadn't seen Jessica in a while and asked, "How are you doing?"

She said, "Great." and asked me, "What have you been up to?"

I told her, "Not too much. I haven't been beaten up by Jorge in a while, and that's been nice."

She laughed, and we joked around for a couple of minutes and sort of flirted.

Jessica was cute, famous, and fun, but I felt a definite connection with Paige. We walked away and talked a little about how she felt the community was doing with Social-Emotional health and how tonight had to help in that respect.

She asked me, "What are you noticing?"

I told her honestly, with the whole Jorge thing, "I haven't had time to just people-watch, and we should make it a point to do that more in the future."

She asked me, "Is that an invitation to hang out more?"

I answered, "Yes, in a professional sense."

We both laughed and continued to joke around and flirt. It was nice. I missed my wife tremendously, but it felt good to connect and have fun with a female. I promised myself I wouldn't do more than just flirt and have some fun, but I couldn't help feeling that Paige felt the same way I did and just flirting may not be enough. For tonight, it was plenty. We had fun, and late into the night, we said good night and headed to our respective huts for the evening.

Chapter Sixteen: Moving forward

The next night, Dr. Linn, Michael, Representative Hix, and Paige stood in front of the rest of the community. Michael and Dr. Linn started off by reviewing what little we knew about why we were here. They both explained, "We don't have many answers, but that can't stop us from moving forward." They talked briefly about the meeting we had with Jorge's community and that right now, "There are two basic camps, and both are developing their own guidelines for the individuals in their camps."

Michael then asked Katie and Hamir to give a summary of what they had found by doing a census.

They quickly explained, "There are 78 in our camp, 19 in Jorge's, and 3 still unaccounted for."

Michael continued, "We have canvased the island, found two individuals dead when we found them, and still had not found one individual."

Colby went over the process we would go through to find out more about the two individuals that were found dead, "But we did not have any more information at that time."

Dr. Linn then explained that during that search, we found out a lot about the island and what resources it had. He continued to identify, "We are on an island, and there are no other signs of other individuals or that other people have ever been on the island. There was fertile land, plenty of fruits and vegetation that could provide for our needs."

He also said there "seemed to be enough birds and fish that we could live a healthy life, probably in fact, healthier than we had before we were "planted" here."

Dr. Linn continued, "In all my dealings with individuals on the island, it, in fact, looks like we are getting healthier."

He used me as an example, stating that, based on my vitals, "Drew actually seems to be getting younger as far as his health is concerned."

I wasn't the only one he had seen this with, but because I was the oldest, he had noticed a significant change in my overall cardiovascular system, "although it could be because I was eating healthier and exercising more, I definitely did not seem to have the body of a 64-year-old."

Michael then told everyone how "The community seems to be adapting to the new environment, and the farmers' market and social events that are occurring show our resiliency and ability to make it in this new world."

He and Dr. Linn concluded, "Although we're not sure why we were here, after an extensive search of the island, we find it has all the things we need to survive and is very livable."

Paige then got up and introduced herself and her qualifications as a Clinical Psychiatrist and went on to conclude how, "I've been observing the various activities and interactions between the inhabitants in the community." She explained that "all individuals seemed to be anxious about the situation, but they were all adapting and functioning as appropriately as possible under the circumstances."

Between the town meetings, the social events, and individual interactions she observed, she felt that "Most individuals were figuring out how to be a productive part of this community."

She was watching how "Most would deal with the loss of people they had loved and "losing" people that had been a big part of their lives" and "Was worried how this might impact us as we moved forward."

She continued, "The lack of knowledge about what actually happened and where these individuals were would always be on our minds, and we needed to make sure we were addressing these feelings in the future with friends we had developed here."

Throughout the presentations, I just watched the crowd. There was a lot of head shaking in agreement with what was being presented. There did seem to be some angst when Colby talked about the deceased and missing individuals; a lot of people looked at each other and wondered what had happened and what Colby might find.

The last part had brought a lot of whispers and individuals talking about what Paige said, and they all seemed to agree that everyone needed to deal with this, and support might be necessary.

I also noticed that Deryl, Peter, and Cheryl had snuck in the back. They were keeping a low profile, but I did notice them listening intently, especially when Colby was discussing the missing #s. I didn't draw any conclusions but made a mental note to talk to Colby about including them in the investigation.

Peter was a police officer and could possibly add some insight to the "crime" scenes, and with them as a part of the process, we could possibly find out if they had any previous knowledge of these individuals. My first encounter with Jorge could have gone south quickly, and if he had met these individuals, who knows what the result might have been?

I also made a mental note to talk to Jessica and find out why she had felt Jorge was attacking her that first evening and what she thought would have happened if I hadn't shown up.

The last part of the town meeting was all Representative Hix. He definitely had a flair for public speaking and had a presence when in front of an audience. He talked about "Representing the people" and "How government sometimes got a bad name, but in essence, it was working for the people, and it was an honor representing the voice of the people," and in our Democratic Republic, "Government might not be perfect, but it did its best to get things right."

He said that, like Paige, he too, had been observing our community and that we needed to start thinking about guidelines that could make sure that all people had a voice and were being represented. He eloquently went on about how this was a chance to "get it right" and have a government that would truly work for the people.

I really thought he was going to sing the Star-Spangled Banner or recite the Pledge of Allegiance; he was so passionate about what he was saying. Representative Hix made sense. We needed to think about who would lead us and what they would decide. Over the next few weeks, we needed to come up with some type of constitution about what we would like to see as far as rules, policies, and laws and how these would be implemented. Although we weren't sure where we were or how long we would be here, it would be prudent to come up with a plan to make sure all individuals had certain rights, but not at the expense of the entire community.

This really got people stirred up. You could see individuals, for the first time, start to think about this long-term. We weren't just here for a short time but might need to look at being a group that needed to not only work together but also think long term on making a community that needed to figure out how to survive indefinitely.

Representative Hix had got the ball rolling and the people in the crowd started to percolate. Individuals started to interject their ideals and "Wanted more individual rights, and not form a government."

It was getting pretty intense when Michael, Dr. Linn, Paige, and Representative Hix came up on stage together and said that these would be items we would be discussing over the next few weeks and everyone would have a say in how this would work. We needed to be civil and do what was best for the entire community, and that would take some time, but all views would be looked at, and decisions would be made after everyone had a voice.

The meeting ended, and like all nights when the community got together, everyone headed to the beach. You could see groups forming and intense discussions taking place. There had been a lot of information, and this was a time for people to get together and process the information.

I decided to try to talk to Jorge's gang. I walked over to Deryl simply to say hi and see how it was going, and I was immediately intercepted aggressively by Peter.

I raised my hands and said I was just saying "Hi" when Cheryl intervened.

She was polite and greeted me with a cold "Hello," as did Deryl.

I asked, "What are your thoughts on the meeting?"

Cheryl let me know, "Our group has already decided a number of things, and we don't feel the two communities had the same ideas."

I said, "I'm not sure I agree, and I would like to continue to discuss some things in the future."

Deryl said, "No one is sure what's going on, we all need to communicate and try to do what is best for everyone that is on the island."

I thought that was thoughtful, and we all just started to talk. Both Deryl and Cheryl were curious about "Whether we would let individuals from our community be a part of theirs."

I responded with the same questions, "Could a person in their community leave and be a part of ours?"

That hung in the air, with no real answer, when Peter asked about the missing people. "What did we know about them, and what were our next steps going to be?"

I told him I was unsure, but I could have Colby meet with him if he was interested in being involved.

Cheryl also wondered, "Where were they found, and was foul play suspected?'

Sort of a weird question, I thought, but I told her I did not know much and we were going to be looking into it in the next few days. If anyone from Jorge's group wanted to be involved, we would reach out.

Peter and Cheryl walked away, and I was standing with Deryl. He asked, "How are you doing, and have you recovered from the beat down I gave you last week?"

He had a smile on his face, and I got the feeling he understood what I was doing during the competition. I told him, "I've had been beaten up a number of times since I arrived on the island, and I haven't kept track of who did the best job of kicking my ass, but you were pretty good, and I wouldn't want to get in a real fight with you."

He was a big boy, and I'm pretty sure he could handle me. Remember those rednecks I had grown up with, Deryl had redneck written all over him, and I couldn't help but feel that he didn't belong in Jorge's gang. It had just happened, and if given the chance, he would like to hang out and just do his thing.

I get the feeling that due to circumstances and where he is in the pecking order of Jorge's gang, this might not be an easy thing to accomplish. If Jorge's gang was like the gangs I'd seen, once you were in the hierarchy, it was hard to get out. Jorge had probably given Deryl a lot of responsibility and trusted him, and Deryl was going to have a hard time getting out of that position.

We said our "goodbyes," and he hurried off to Cheryl and Peter to head back to their camp and let Jorge know what they had found out.

Down on the beach, Dr. Linn, representative Hix, Michael, Colby, and Paige were going over their thoughts on the meeting.

I interrupted to let them know, "I just talked to Deryl and Cheryl, and they might know something or at least would like to help out in the investigation of the missing people."

I told Colby it was up to him how he wanted to proceed, but they did seem interested in being part of the investigation. Colby pondered that information and said he would "think about it but had reservations."

I then just sat and listened to the group reflect on what they had just learned. I found it interesting although I wasn't involved in the presentation, they allowed me to listen in. No one else was there, and I was #98. I used to be a high school principal, yet I was part of the "leadership" team that was determining the future of our community. I didn't say much; just listened and took it all in. I would be doing a lot of that over the next few weeks, and it helped me to understand the complex process we would be navigating to determine the future of our community.

Chapter Seventeen: #21 = Deryl Walker

#21's name was Deryl Walker. He was 6"4" and weighed around three hundred pounds. Some of it flab, but most muscle he had developed over the years as a welder. He grew up in the blue-collar community of Wheeling, West Virginia. It was known for its steel mills and the people that worked in them. They were tough, worked long eight-hour days, sometimes double shifts, and had fun on weekends. Wheeling and the tri-state area of Eastern Ohio, Western Pennsylvania, and West Virginia had suffered since the 1990s, and Deryl had to learn to be resilient and find work wherever he could. He was known in Wheeling for his tough, hard-nosed attitude and willingness to do dirty jobs others wouldn't. He had a big extended family, and everyone in his tight-knit neighborhood knew the Walkers and trusted and respected the name.

When Deryl was "planted," he was alone and wandering the beach. A tough-looking Latino had come out of the woods with two other people and started hassling him. At first, he just brushed it off, but after they kept it up, he grabbed one of the individuals who was with the Latino and threw him against a tree. He then looked at the other two individuals and asked, "Anyone else want a part of me?"

He was in a place he'd never seen, surrounded by three people he'd never met and wasn't going to take any of their shit. A guy with the #6 on his shirt stepped up and introduced himself. He said, "I've just got on this island and am trying to find individuals to figure out what is going on and see if they are willing to work with me?"

He would offer protection, and they could all try to come up with a plan to survive. Jorge continued to explain, "We don't know why we're here or where here is, but I came from an environment where we had to survive, and we could sure use a big body like you."

Deryl calmed down, and Jorge continued to sell Deryl the reasons he should join his gang. Jorge saw that Deryl was big, could handle himself, and would be a good addition to his group.

Deryl agreed, and as he got more involved in Jorge's gang, Jorge gave him more responsibility. Deryl and Jorge became friends, and they worked together to make sure the people in their gang followed their rules and helped support the community they were developing.

He didn't always agree with Jorge's methods but had the status that people respected him and followed Jorge's lead because it made things easier. He had seen some individuals not be supportive of Jorge, and they had got their ass kicked, hard.

Although he could take care of himself, he didn't need the headache of fighting others because Jorge was angry, and he had seen that occasionally. The gang started to develop a culture that mirrored things he had read about gangs in the real world. They had an initiation, where new members had to prove themselves by taking on three or four other members in an all-out brawl. He has seen some members get pretty messed up, and he would never take part in the initiations.

The competitions were a way to see who they had to worry about and how they could control them, and Deryl thought they were stupid. Jorge, due to his ultimate fighting skills, and Deryl, because of his size and strength, were the two toughest, and if someone tried to move up the ladder, one of those two would take them on in a challenge and put them in their place.

As they spent more time on the island, Deryl saw drugs and alcohol become more a part of their culture. Deryl was pretty strait-laced and didn't partake but had to admit the culture was loose, and there weren't a lot of rules they had to follow, and because of the relationship he had with Jorge, he had it pretty easy.

After the outsiders had come into the camp, he realized there could be other things he could be doing, and there were other individuals out there that he could fraternize with.

Jorge's group was starting to scare him a little, and Jorge had changed ever since Cheryl came along. He liked that Jorge trusted him and the status he had in the gang, but he thought it might be time to move on. He just wasn't sure how Jorge would take it and what the consequences might be.

This whole murder thing was scary, and he felt that his group could earn some credibility by helping out, and ultimately, they could work with the other communities that were developing in this new world. It wouldn't be easy, but maybe he could use his relationship with Jorge to build bridges with the outsiders.

Chapter Eighteen: Where are we now?

The next day, I sought out Jessica. I wanted to get her thoughts on that first day and her thoughts on Jorge and if she felt he could be involved in the missing #s. I found her hanging out with Don, Jessie, and Louis out in the jungle. They were sitting around with a couple of other females: Zenaida, whom Jessica had befriended earlier, Tanver, the environmental scientist, and the two runners Hayley and Kerri. They evidently had formed a small group that liked to hang out together.

I hadn't been aware of Jessica's passion for the environment, and the group she surrounded herself with shared that same passion. They were all into the environment back in the "old world" and were working with Don and Jessie to form a type of farm that could help sustain and improve our living conditions while at the same time being environmentally safe for the future.

Jessica and Tanver were talking and said, "By planning out where we are going to plant and the type of crops we will harvest, we could do a great job of efficiently farming for years to come."

Don was interested and asked, "How can we farm the crops we need and at the same time conserve the land we are using?"

I listened to the conversation and was impressed by the plan they were developing. Don had a strong background in farming, and Tanver had some great ideas on how to harvest the crops and keep the soil and land from being depleted. Jessica seemed to be leading the group and had some strong opinions on these issues and made sure the group heard her. I hadn't seen that side of her but was impressed with her knowledge and willingness to listen to Don and Tanver about how to proceed.

After a while, the group turned to me and asked me if I had any thoughts on the issue. I responded, "I grew up on a farm, and my dad was always moving crops based on the impact they had on the soil. This wasn't new but was more intense than anything my dad had done."

I took the time to change the subject and checked to see if everyone was on the same page about the history of the island and what was taking place. I had been with the leadership team and was curious how much everyone knew about everything that had been happening on the island.

We started with everyone explaining how and where they had been "planted." We found that we had landed all over and that it seemed very random, and no one could see a relationship to who landed where. Jessica shared her experience with Jorge and I and told everyone it was "terrifying and confusing."

She joked about an "old guy" coming up to "save her" and getting his ass kicked. She did go on to say that I distracted Jorge enough that she could get away and appreciated that.

Then, individuals started talking about the first people they encountered and where that had happened. Again, no patterns could be seen. Individuals just happened on to others by chance. Some decided to band together, others did their own thing. Zenaida and Jessica had a group of about 9-10 people that had a camp about a mile from the beach. They both felt "the group had a great vibe, and they felt safe and secure when they were with their friends."

They decided early to band together to give them strength in numbers and found each one had a unique talent to help them survive. They had a lot of questions, but over time had pretty much determined to make this place as livable as possible and roll with living here.

Tanver chimed in that "she and about 10-12 other like-minded individuals had done the same thing."

Most of these individuals had some type of science background and had met and banded together. They found a safe spot that had the necessary resources to survive and provided safety and had similar experiences to Jessica's group.

The science group was probably the most enterprising group, always looking for ways to improve their overall living conditions and having the smarts to do it. They knew enough about the environment we were in to figure out ways to make this world more livable. Both groups, along with Don, Jessie, and Louis, explained they were comfortable with the people they had met, and everything seemed to be working out. They had visited each other's camp, and some were talking about relocating but weren't sure yet.

We then started talking about the beach. Some people were thinking about relocating down there, and hopefully, others would too, and there would be greater safety in numbers. They figured with Michael, Colby, and other authority-like figures it could promote a safer environment. Hayley and Kerri told the group they had, "stumbled upon four other such camps. All were in the vicinity of fresh water and fish, and all had around 5-10 individuals in each camp, and all were self-sufficient and seemed to have generally positive relationships within them."

Hayley and Kerri, the runners, had the most contact with the different groups and, at one time or another, spent time in each camp. They related that the consistent message was, "No one knew why we were here, but they were going to make the best of it."

All the different areas had developed water and food gathering strategies that helped them get the basic needs, and all were within a 2–5-mile radius of the beach. They found it interesting the variety of ways different groups had made it work, but when it came right down to it, "Most individuals found a group of people they trusted and were able to live with."

Tanver mentioned, "The environment was great for finding the necessary resources to ensure we all had the means to stay healthy and safe." She added, "It was almost like someone didn't want us to struggle too much with the primary needs, and everything has been provided so we wouldn't have to struggle much to survive."

No one had encountered any dangerous wildlife or poisonous vegetation, and there were enough fish and fowl to sustain a healthy community.

The different groups, although living in different areas, seemed to get along, although other than the beach, they didn't co-mingle too much. Hayley and Kerri both said that everyone they came into contact with "Had been nice and willing to share."

They agreed, "There's a different vibe with Jorge's gang, and they tended to stay away from that area."

One time, when they did run in that area, a number of Jorge's gang watched them closely, and "it seemed creepy, and we were wary of them, and they were not as open and friendly as the other groups."

They weren't afraid but concerned about the way they were talked to and how the group had a threatening nature to them.

It was interesting to get a history of how we all came to inhabit the various parts of the island and the relationships that were being developed. The more we talked, the more we realized that almost everything that had happened up to this point was by chance. The circumstances of where we were "planted" and the proximity of where we were dropped had a huge impact on our current situation.

Except for Jessica and me. I reiterated the whole Jorge situation and how "I was a little gun shy of finding other individuals and had made it a point to hide as far away from the beach as possible."

I had become a loner and was concerned that there could be other aggressive individuals who were not willing to work together and, therefore chose to build a camp and prepare for the worst. Once I was safe, I then chose to go out and try to find if anyone else was around that I could work with to survive. I told them how Don, Jessie and Louis had tried to trap me and scare me, and that didn't help, and we all laughed at this and started to have a little fun.

This had been an enlightening experience and we continued to have some fun and make friendships. Towards the end of the night, I asked Jessica, "Can we talk?

She had been engaged with the group the whole evening, and she seemed to get along with everyone. I finally recognized her for a role she was famous for on TV, and throughout the night, everyone kidded with her on being the biggest celebrity on the island, and if we ever did return to the "real world" if they could get a pen and paper, they wanted her autograph. She took the kidding well and seemed nice and people seemed to respect her for the way she treated others, even if she was famous.

As we moved from the group, Jessica and I started to talk about the first night and why she was so afraid of Jorge. I asked if he aggressively threatened and attacked her. What had happened that evening before I got involved? She told me, "Nothing happened other than that I had just found myself in a completely foreign environment, and a big Latino guy with tattoos approached me." She had just "Overreacted to the situation."

When I asked if she felt he was capable of killing someone, she didn't have an answer. Other than her observing him beating the crap out of me twice, she didn't see him do anything in their first meeting to say he was capable of killing her.

If I thought Jorge were the killer, Jessica's take hadn't convinced me; in fact, I was more convinced he wasn't a killer, but who was? We talked a little more and said our goodbyes.

Today was a learning experience and I had a pretty good understanding of most of the inhabitants on the island. I hadn't met them all, but the ones I had, I walked away with the same feeling I had previously. I respected these individuals and felt they would work well together, and we could make this new world a good place to live until we figured out everything.

Chapter Nineteen: #32 = Jessica Morgan

#32 was Jessica Morgan. She was a strong-willed individual who had made a name for herself in the last 20 or so years. She always did the talk show circuit, was in a bunch of "not quite" famous movies, and had quite the following on Twitter and Instagram. Jessica was a beautiful young lady. She had a body that would stop traffic and a positive, bubbly personality that people were drawn to. Over the years, she had been a permanent part of the tabloid scene and was watched closely by all the magazines.

From what you saw on TV, you saw a really neat young lady who had navigated Hollywood as well as anyone and had an amazing career. The tabloids were always meddling into her private life, but she was a private person, and really, no one needed to know about her private life. If they wanted to try to make every public viewing with a male a major event, she couldn't care less.

She had learned a long time ago that her confidence was her strongest asset, and she would be damned if the press would affect her, no matter what they said. She had a lot of friends in the business and had spent years cultivating relationships that would help her career in the future.

Jessica had a good head on her shoulders and had always worked to make good decisions concerning her career and future. All the same, Jessica was here. She didn't know where here was, but she was going to do her best to get back to California and work on some projects she had in the work with some of her friends.

She had to admit this was confusing, and after the first night and the fiasco she had with #6 and #98, she was still trying to wrap her head around where she was and what had happened literally the second she had arrived. The Latino guy scared her to death. She had just been "planted," and all of a sudden, a tall, tatted-up Latino came out of nowhere and got too close. She freaked out and started screaming, and then this old guy came out of the woods and started yelling. The whole thing was out of a bad movie, and she had one of the leading roles. Now, the old guy and the Latino guy are both players on the island, and she is trying to figure out her role in the whole scenario.

Jessica had hung out on the beach after being "planted" and approached the first two people she saw after the first night. The girl had recognized her and was so excited she wet her pants. When the guy realized who she was and they started talking, everything sort of fit into place. The man had #57 on and was named Hakeem; the female was #78, and her name *was Zenaida. Hakeem had been a college soccer player at North Carolina and had an excellent career before graduating and becoming a coach. He hadn't been quite good enough to play professionally and had decided to move on with his life and quit following his boyhood dream. Zenaida had become a college English professor, had completed her doctorate in Early English Literature, and had just become tenured at a small liberal arts school, Carnegie Mellon, in Pittsburg. After talking with Jessica, they agreed to hide out just off the beach and see what happened.*

They had, like the other groups, developed certain routines that allowed them to feel safe and secure. They had built a shelter and found water and fruit to keep them safe and fed. As time progressed, they made a variety of friends and developed some pretty solid relationships since being "planted."

After the conch meeting, they began to network and found others to hang with close to the beach. They had met Bob early and enjoyed having another male to provide security, although Jessica and Zenaida could take care of themselves, they found there was strength in numbers until they figured things out.

At the shindig, she had talked to Don, Jessie, and Louis and developed an interest in the farm and how to help the entire community. They were becoming a fixture in that area as of late.

Chapter Twenty: The plot thickens

When I got back to the camp on the beach, I found out that a group had decided to travel to the sights where the bodies had been found. Brodie and Louis, who were part of the original search team, would lead them to the sights of the victims. Colby, Dr. Linn and Valerie Chen, the lawyer, would go with him and see what they could get from the "crime scenes." All three of these individuals had experience in crime scenes, and they didn't want too many people contaminating the area. To my surprise, I found out that Dave Valesky, the policeman and Cheryl Thiel, the model, both from Jorge's group, had asked to be included. Dave, I understood, but why Cheryl? I didn't see how a model could have a lot of investigative skills and how she was going to aid in this process.

When I asked Colby about this, his response was that "Jorge had chosen these two because they wanted to make sure his gang wasn't accused of something, just because of their reputation, and these two individuals were going to make sure this didn't happen."

The investigative team left, and the talk at the farmers market revolved around whether they would find anything and "Were these individuals killed or had they just been the unfortunate victims of an awful accident?"

I went back up to Don and Jessie's farm and started to work on clearing some land and planting some crops. When I got there, I saw that Soni, Tanver, Hayley and Kerri were already present and helping clear the land. Don had developed some tools. Although you would be hard-pressed to call them that. We had no metal, so the tools were made of wood and stone. Breaking through the sod and turning over the soil were challenging obstacles that everyone there had to take part in. Getting the soil ready for even a row of beans took all day, and it took everyone working with their hands and sub-standard tools to do it. Luckily the ground was fertile, and after you broke through the sod, it wasn't too difficult to turn the soil.

Soni, the master gardener, Ivan, the horticulturalist, Don and Tanver had worked to get seeds from the crops they had come across on the island and had worked to make sure they had seeds that would grow in this environment. They had harvested some tubers, small potatoes that had lots of eyes, and decided they would be easiest to plant. Tubers had a history of growing quickly and getting a bountiful harvest. Tanver had chitted them and left them in the sunlight to ensure they had enough eyes and were ready to plant.

As the farm hands turned the soil, Don followed and placed the tubers in the ground and covered them with soil. We marked the rows and continued to plant. Tanver had tomatoes, cucumber, peppers, corn, and lettuce that she and others in their group had located. She and Soni had worked to cultivate the necessary seeds, and she, Soni, Ivan and Don had planned how to plant them most efficiently to ensure the maximum harvest.

They were the brains of the operation, and we had about 6 "farm hands" to do the physical labor. It took over two weeks, but in that time, we had planted beans, tomatoes, potatoes, peppers, lettuce, corn, carrots, and cucumbers. Tanver and Selina Hernandez, the dietician, felt this would be a good start to balancing the diet of the community. That, along with all the natural fruits we could find, provided a healthy diet for everyone and a consistent source of food for the groups.

I'm not going to lie; using rocks and limbs to break ground sucked and was hard work, but a lot of individuals heard about it, and it ended up being a neat experience. Many inhabitants who didn't do the work ended up coming up in the evenings and providing meals and spirits to say thank you. Those three weeks were hard work, but they brought much of the community together and hopefully prepared us for a better tomorrow.

Like many things, I noticed, was that with a community of 70 people, no one was forced to do anything; everyone just pitched in, and a real feeling of togetherness was developing. I wouldn't say we partied each night; our hands and knees hurt too much, but we did have old-fashioned gatherings and got to know more people. As word traveled, some nights, as many as 40 people would show up just to show their appreciation for the work that was being done. In the true spirit of community, all would bring something to the table, and you could see a strong sense of accomplishment was being established.

Back on the beach, the investigating team was returning, and everyone wanted to know what they found out. Colby and Dr. Linn met with Michael and Paige to share the information and figure out the next steps. Michael asked me to drop by due to my working with Deryl and Jorge's gang to listen and possibly offer some insight. Over the months, Michael had begun talking to me more and more and trusted my view on things. He and Paige had had some conversations and felt I was a good listener and had gotten around to a broad range of individuals, and most seemed to respect my common sense and level-headedness. They felt that my being a part of the group that was determining what was going on could add some credibility. I was honored and did what I always tried to do, listen to understand, gather as much information as possible and work with others to make an informed decision.

Colby started off by explaining, "We cordoned off the area and looked over the area before anyone else."

He then explained he "Brought Dave in to discuss and confirm his findings."

Both had experience in crime scene investigation, and they would talk about what they considered evidence. They closely looked at the area and the perimeter. They were looking for anything that was out of the ordinary. Footprints, signs of an altercation, disrupted plants, soil, etc. They quickly looked at the body to see if there was any evidence of a fight or confrontation.

Once they had that information/evidence, they brought in Dr. Linn to look at the body and make his assessment of the cause of death. Dr. Linn was there just to do an unofficial autopsy to see if he could determine the cause of death. There were limited tools he had at his disposal; it pretty much came down to his looking at the corpse and determining if the cause of death was from natural causes or was suspicious. They followed this process at each crime scene.

#100 was unclear. Dr. Linn determined that the death was caused by the fall. That much was clear, but Colby and Dave felt that someone else was in that area. They could not ascertain that the person was in the vicinity at the same time or not, but there were some indications that some type of altercation might have occurred. Both agreed that there was some plant and soil disruption close enough to the edge of the cliff that two people could have struggled, but they could not say for sure. More forensic evidence was needed, and they simply didn't have the equipment to make a definitive statement that it was murder. There were enough questions to make them skeptical, but they couldn't be sure.

#49 was a different story. Colby looked over the scene and then had Dave do a sweep. When both were done, Colby asked Dr. Linn to look at the body. He asked Dave to share what he saw. Both agreed that "there had been a struggle."

It seemed that from the evidence, one person had approached #49 from behind. A struggle occurred, evidenced by the disruption of the soil and plants in the area. And #49's neck had been snapped, and there were marks around his neck. The neck being snapped might not have killed #49 automatically, but disabled him. Colby and Dave both agreed that "someone that could snap an individual's neck had to have some pretty intense training in the area of martial arts or at least some type of experience in how to complete the action."

Either way, once the person had been immobilized, there was evidence to suggest that the individual had continued to strangle #49, as indicated by the marks around his neck. Dr. Linn could not confirm that #49 had died from a broken neck or from strangulation. Again, due to lack of necessary tools to complete an autopsy, no clear conclusion could be rendered. The conclusion was that someone had attacked #49 from behind, disabled him with a violent movement to his neck area, and then killed him by strangling him when he was unconscious.

No one said anything. It scared the hell out of me, and I'm sure the rest had the same feeling. Someone had been killed on this island. Someone on this island killed someone, maybe two people, and they were still out there. Was it the missing #51? Was it Jorge which some evidence pointed to? Or was another killer among us, and we didn't know who it was?

The other question looming was, do we tell the rest of the community what we found? Dave and Cheryl had left when the investigation team returned. What were they sharing with Jorge? We had the facts, but no one was willing to assess the situation. There were too many questions. Jorge automatically jumped to the head of the list, but who was going to question him, and what would those questions look like? Was he the only person that had these skills?

The island, although presenting a lot of questions, had been a safe place up till now. Suddenly, this was going to bring up a lot of concerns within both communities. Michael was not crazy about sharing this information with everyone. He said, "It would cause alarm, and people would be afraid, and they had enough going on that they didn't need to know about this."

Dr. Linn agreed. Paige was on the fence. She understood where Michael was coming from but was concerned that if the rest of the community found out, it would be hard to earn their trust in the future.

Colby was clear, "We can't tell people; we will quietly do an investigation, and if the person didn't know we knew, we would have a better chance of finding out who it was."

To me, the answer was clear, "we have to tell everyone. We have to be honest, and people need to be able to help us investigate. These people lived with whoever had done this. They might have some information we could use."

We also had to ensure Dave and Cheryl would inform Jorge's gang. We wouldn't accuse anyone; we would just give them the facts and work with Jorge's gang to devise a plan to investigate. We had a problem, a BIG problem, and we had to meet it head-on. Hiding it from the community could only lead to distrust. We needed to use them as a part of the solution and not part of the problem.

Colby didn't like It, but we decided that Dr. Linn, Paige and I would inform our community at a town meeting we would call for tomorrow night. We would give them the facts and tell them to be careful. We weren't accusing anyone, but if anyone had heard anything, let Colby or Michael know.

Michael and Colby would go over to Jorge's gang and talk to Jorge and Dave and get their thoughts on how this should be investigated. The rest of the night, we discussed a plan. Telling our community was going to cause anxiety, but I was really concerned about how Jorge and his gang would respond and was happy I didn't have to go to that meeting.

All the evidence pointed to Jorge; he was aggressive and strong, had Ultimate Fighting experience and demonstrated a mean streak when frustrated. We aren't sure what led to this act, but Jorge had the skill and temperament to pull it off. I'd seen him in action and seen the rage in his face when I wouldn't come out of the water. This wasn't a stretch for me to believe he had killed someone; it could have been me.

Another day, another crisis. I sort of liked the idea of just working on the farm and not worrying about all these situations. These meetings did give me a chance to visit Paige more, and I kinda liked that. After our leadership meeting, we hung out and processed the news of the day.

She had agreed with me about letting the rest of our community know what was going on and told me, "You working on the farm has given you a lot of credibility, and I think most people like you, even if you are #98." She smiled with that last statement and followed it up with, "I think you should at least be #54."

We both laughed, and I said, "I thought my work and effort at least should get me #69."

That got a laugh, and she went on to get serious and explained how "I feel sorry for everyone being "planted" on a deserted island without any explanation. Being torn from their family and friends is bad enough, but now to possibly have a murderer on the loose in their community is making what was hard even harder."

We both agreed that most of the people we had met were good people and us being honest with them would be the best route. As always, we would work with them, support them as best we could, and hope for the best. I couldn't help but feel every time we took a couple of steps forward, something always had us take a step back. Someone or something seemed to be testing us, testing our resiliency and metal as individuals. I couldn't escape what

Kiran had said about the "AI and how they were curious about human behavior and resiliency."

141

Chapter Twenty-One: #16 =
Colby Miller

#16, Colby Miller had been a decorated FBI agent. He had been involved in a number of high-level investigations and was known for his tough and unrelenting style of getting to the bottom of things. He was intense, some would say too intense, but he was thorough, honest and fair. He went with his gut a lot but had been in the business long enough to sort through the crap. Other agents respected him, but he had pissed enough of his bosses off that he probably wasn't going to get those promotions he deserved.

Colby just was "planted" in the middle of the jungle one day. He remembered he had been working on a murder case in downtown Memphis, and the next thing he knew, he was on a tropical island with a bunch of people he'd never met. The people he had encountered were nice, and they seemed to have good heads on their shoulders, but it was still unclear why he was there. He tried to use his investigative skills to figure out why we were here, but there were no clues, and he'd be damned if he could come up with any reason to be here.

Now he was involved in a murder investigation on a deserted island with 100, make that 98 people. He didn't have the equipment, just his mind, and everyone was looking to him to solve a murder that there were very few clues to. The crime scenes gave him very little information, he didn't have fingerprint analysis or crime scene technology. Hell, he couldn't even get a time of death, let alone a cause of death.

He'd always told himself that police investigation was 40% hard work and tracking down leads, 40% what his gut told him and 20% crime scene evidence. Lately, with all the advances in DNA research and forensic science, he wasn't so sure about those percentages. Still, in this case, he was working on it. He could forget about forensic science and get down to good old-fashioned police work. Checking on leads, interrogating witnesses and figuring out who dun it. He liked that and looked forward to using his police skills to find out who was behind these murders.

He didn't say it out loud but felt both #100 and #49 had been murdered. There was just something about the crime scenes that said this might be a sociopath. This was a person who seemed charming and charismatic on the surface but had a total disregard for rules and other people's feelings. They were narcissistic and, consistently exhibited dishonest behavior, and didn't care what others thought. They were hard to identify, especially if they had practiced these behaviors for a long period of time. They often came off as helpful and liked to be around the scenes they had created but were almost playing a game with the police. The trick was not to let them know that you suspected them, and they ultimately would make a mistake, and you could catch them.

This case on the island was interesting; five people had gone to the crime scene, and three actually showed some signs of being a sociopath. Louis, the guy who had helped lead them to the scene, was an interesting character. There was something about him that didn't fit. He said he was a stockbroker but didn't show a good grasp of how stocks and bonds worked. In casual conversation, he was kind of a bullshitter and talked in circles. In a quick look, he noticed that Louis's feet were similar in size to those at the crime scene. He couldn't be sure but had decided the prints left at both crime scenes were a man's footprint. There were some definite red flags he would have to look into.

The police officer, Dave Valesky, from Jorge's gang, seemed sincere enough. He definitely knew his way around a crime scene and had a good nose for what to look for. It almost seemed he was trying too hard to point the blame at his boss, Jorge. He was always referencing his fighting skills and how mean he could be. He didn't come right out and say it, but he threw Jorge under the bus every chance he got.

The last one was a mystery. He wasn't sure why Cheryl had come. She was hot, a model and, from all indications, someone to be wary of. It didn't take long to find out she had an attitude, and when she felt Dave was saying too much, she told him, "Shut up. You need to keep quiet and not talk so much."

When she spoke, he listened and said nothing about Jorge when she was close by. She was a manipulator; she liked to be in control and made it clear that the police had never been fair to Jorge in his past, and she was not going to allow them to mistreat him now. She was not a police lover. They were arrogant assholes that didn't have to follow the rules, and she was there to make sure no one was unjustly accused, and the evidence was looked at fairly. She had no skill in the area of police work and clearly was there to protect Jorge from being unfairly judged.

All of these individuals were persons of interest, and they, along with Jorge, would have to be questioned, and Colby would have to use his skills as a detective to see if any of them were the killer.

Whether in the past world or in this one, Colby was dealing with things he knew. He was excited to use his knowledge and skill to figure out what was going on and do it quickly so everyone could move forward and meet the challenges of this new world without two murders hanging over their heads.

Chapter Twenty-Two: A glimpse into the future

Representative Hix started looking at developing a guiding document. He had an open meeting where Bob, the Real Estate Agent. Zenaida, an English professor. Arianna Rachkowski, an Architect, Brodie, the ex-marine and four other individuals signed up. Being an old History teacher, I volunteered to be a part of it also. The people on the committee had mostly positive experiences with our lives in the United States, and it was clear from the start we would use the Constitution and Declaration of Independence as our guiding documents.

Two of the individuals were from the business world. Mark Walden, #89 and Elon Witosky, #58, wanted to make sure that the government didn't get involved in the farmers' market we had started and didn't want the government interfering in the free market. We thought that was farther down the line and didn't really want to get into that discussion yet.

We all agreed we had come from a place where polarizing opinions dominated the government but wanted to stay away from divisive ideologies until we had a chance to develop as a community. It would be a scaled-down version, and we would adjust what we put into it to fit a community of 100. We started with individual rights; there was a strong sentiment that individuals should be in control of their lives and certain freedoms should be guaranteed.

Brodie introduced the idea of developing some type of military in case of conflict, but we decided to table that till we could have more discussion. Most agreed that individuals should be able to choose where they wanted to live, and all should have basic rights like freedom of speech and movement throughout the island.

Then, the question of laws and rules came up. If we found out who killed the two individuals, what would happen? Was it an eye for an eye? What was the punishment? What about Jorge's gang? If they infringed on our rights, what would happen? What if Jorge's gang didn't agree? Who would enforce these laws? Would we have police? What would their responsibilities be? How were we going to decide who would be the police? After three hours or so, we realized this was a tall order, and we should model a lot of what we did around the US Constitution. We had to think about our situation, develop the guidelines and determine what made sense. We made simple, broad rights and could add as the situation dictated. And determining a format for decision-making in the future.

They were:

1. Freedom to speak freely.
2. Freedom to move where they wanted and live where they wanted.
3. Freedom of religion, individuals could choose to worship where and how they wanted but could not infringe on others.
4. As laws were established, all individuals would have the right to have a trial of their peers if there was a dispute.
5. Due Process would be accorded for any individual who broke the law.
6. Individuals could be required to work for the "government" in extreme emergencies.

This was put in place if there was an emergency where we needed individuals to work together to work through difficult times and support each other.

7. All individuals were expected to work for the good of the community.

This was put in place to ensure everyone knew they had a responsibility to support each other throughout the community.

We also determined that there would be 7 at-large openings for our Congress. Individuals would run for these positions, and everyone would have a vote. These people would represent the will of the people and provide input to the governing body. That would be the ruling Senate; there were to be three members of the community elected to make decisions concerning everyday situations that needed to be completed. Ten people, 10% of the population, would represent the other 90. We thought this was a fair balance and would look at a system of checks and balances for the future.

It was a start and did not address the rules that would govern the community. We knew these guidelines were sure to spark discussion throughout the community, and we figured that the Congress and Senate could make those decisions as the community grew. Then there was the question of how Jorge's gang would respond to these ideas. As we continued to talk, we realized what a huge undertaking this was going to be, and a lot of it would be a work in progress.

The underlying question was, what would we do if we found out someone on the island had committed the murders we were investigating? What punishment would we have, and who would carry it out? We knew this would create a lot of discussion based on the views of the community. These hard decisions would ultimately determine the strength of our community and its willingness to move forward.

Chapter Twenty-Three: Suspense and confusion

There was a lot to talk about at the town meeting. Everyone had gathered and understood that information about the missing individuals and an update on the governing process was on the agenda. We had a small community, and word traveled fast and for a meeting like this, everyone would likely be in attendance.

Before Michael got up to start the meeting, there was a buzz throughout the crowd. We weren't sure, but it seemed like there was something in the air, and Paige said, "It seems like the crowd is on edge."

I agreed and said, "It feels like everyone is anxious, and something is going on."

Michael went on and started the meeting with, "Here is Colby Miler. He is going to give us an update on our investigation."

Colby explained what the search team had found and was expanding on the information when Erin Lindt, #34, a Constitutional lawyer, got up and told Colby, "Someone else was missing. #75, Colleen Gillotti, an administrative assistant for Amazon, has been missing since the previous evening."

She was part of Erin's camp, and they had not seen her for two days. It was not like Colleen to not be in camp. She was a good person, and it was not like her leaving camp without telling someone, and it was certainly not in her character to be out overnight. She had a close group of friends, and they had not seen her in two days.

Then another individual stood up, and an electrician, Chris Spatz, #43, explained a guy in their camp was also missing. "Doug Vogel, #25, a Geologist from Cleveland, has been missing for three days now."

Doug had been looking for a particular rock specimen for the last few weeks, trying to develop stronger tools from metamorphic rocks, known to be the hardest rocks in the world. He had helped develop the tools used on the farm for planting and was trying to improve the tools for future use. "The last time we saw him, he had been going out to gather samples."

He had been in the scientist's camp since it started, but no one had seen him since the day before yesterday. Like Colleen, it was uncharacteristic for Doug to just up and leave, and they were concerned that something might have happened to him.

You could feel the chill in the air after Erin and Chris had shared these two people who were missing. We had just found out that a person might have been murdered, and now two other people were missing.

Anxiety gripped the crowd, and Colby did his best to calm them down, but this was crazy. "What was going on?"

Paige took this time to get up and do her best to identify ways to deal with these events. She explained, "We weren't sure Colleen and Pat were dead. There could be a rational reason for them being missing."

She continued, "Just in case, we all need to partner up and make sure we are always with someone. Each small community needs to take precautions about when people come and go."

The community had to work together and find answers to these questions. Were they just lost and missing, or had something happened to them, and we had more mysteries on our hands?

Needless to say, we didn't get to the whole government thing, and a panic was developing. That night, Colby was about ready to lose it. #51 was still missing, and now two others had come up missing. If this was a sociopath, this community would be in trouble. That was five people that were possibly dead because of some crazy person in our midst. We had to solve this fast, or there could be more missing people and individuals in the community could really suffer anxiety and loss.

It was bad enough we were stranded on this island, and people had to deal with that. Now, we had people missing, and it was one more thing that created stress and anxiety in the group of people who had already had enough.

The first three individuals no one had really known, but in this case, these two people had friends. The community knew them, and they were part of it. This is not good, and we need to figure out what is happening.

Groups started to form, and the discussion revolved around staying safe. Community members were making plans with friends and acquaintances to buddy up and go to every place together. Others were talking about developing search parties to see if they could find Colleen and Pat. There was a strong movement to move everyone to the housing that was on the beach and develop a plan to ensure everyone would be safe until we could figure this out.

This is when some type of leadership is necessary, just to offer direction to individuals looking for some. Paige again took the lead. She continued to make sure everyone had someone to go home with tonight. Tomorrow, we would work as a community to develop a plan to figure out what we could do to ensure everyone's safety and find out what was really going on.

Colby, Michael, Dr. Linn, and I walked around to each group and talked over the plan for the night. There was strength in numbers, and all the different communities should go back together and make sure everyone was safe and had a partner to stay with. We couldn't address the elephant in the room, that someone in our midst might be the person that is responsible for all of this, and that was the scariest part.

As people dispersed, I walked up to Paige. I asked her, "What are your plans for tonight?"

I was concerned for the community, and I was especially concerned for her and wanted to make sure she was safe. I didn't know if she was dating anyone and didn't want to be too forward, but I was worried and wanted to make sure she was safe. She answered, "Just heading back to my hut. Would you care to join me?" and gave me a quick wink.

I wouldn't say I was stunned. Pleasantly surprised would be more like it. When I offered to walk her back to her place on the beach, she gladly accepted.

It had been a hell of a day. From the government discussion to the new information about the two missing individuals, a lot of thought had been put into the day, and I was exhausted. At the same time, we had a crisis and not a lot of time to figure out what was going on before the whole community imploded.

Paige and I were a lot alike. We both had analytical sides that kicked in when things got out of control. Instead of running around looking for answers, we both sat down and looked at what we could do rationally to help the situation. On our walk home, we started to analyze the events of the evening and what the plan should be moving forward. First, we looked at the information. We were already missing one individual. Now, two others had come up missing. We had two others that had been murdered, or at least that was the theory we were working from, and someone on the island had committed the murders.

We didn't go down the road that whoever put us on this island was messing with us, although the thought had crossed both our minds. When we got back to her place, we brought up the idea of Jorge's gang and could they be trying to cause confusion and offer a safe place for our community to go. We had not heard if anyone from Jorge's gang was missing, but they were a pretty tight-knit group and probably wouldn't share if someone was. They could also have taken #51, Colleen and Pat and were forcing them to be a part of their gang. We didn't trust Jorge but felt we hadn't seen any behavior from his group that would lead us to believe they were trying to sabotage our group.

The more we talked we kept coming back to there was a murderer among us. I brought up to Paige that "Everyone we have met seems to be above average in their previous job," I went on to say, "They worked hard, made good decisions and had generally been successful in their past."

Jorge was a criminal, but a good criminal. He was good at being a gang member, dealing with the police and his competition and figuring out how not to get caught. Then I brought up the theory that "Maybe we were dealing with another type of criminal. A sociopath, as Colby suggested, and this person was very good at being a sociopath."

Paige had worked with her share of sociopathic personalities. They were smart, deceptive, lied without any kind of tell, and if they were good at it, hard to catch. Paige admitted that "If this was the case and this was an above average sociopath, we would need all our resources to find him before he killed again."

This scared us to death, but it seemed plausible.

I then asked, "Do you see any similarities in the missing people?"

She looked at me quizzically, and I pointed out the pattern; "#100 had been the first to go, then #49 and #51 were missing or dead, now #75 and 25."

When I put it that way, she gasps and realized after #100, the other two pairs added up to 100. Someone was targeting individuals based on the number they were wearing. I didn't want to worry her, but I then pointed out, "We were #98 and her #2."

We decided we needed to be very careful until this person was caught. For the first time, I saw a little bit of panic in Paige's eyes; this was becoming very real very quickly, and she wasn't sure she was ready for it.

I walked her to her hut and informed her, "I will be staying the night; I won't try anything, and I will sleep on the floor."

I'm not sure she liked what I said, but I just wanted to make sure she was all right and could hopefully get a good night's sleep. We cuddled for a while, and I gotta tell you, it felt great, especially under the circumstances, but ultimately, I moved down to the floor because I was afraid of what might happen if I stayed in bed with her.

Chapter Twenty-Four: Who can you trust?

The next morning, the beach area was a hub of activity. Colby and Brodie were organizing search teams, and Dr. Linn and Kim were coming up with a check-in system for residents of the community, a way to keep tabs on if anyone went missing.

They wanted Michael, Val and I to go over to Jorge's camp and inform them of the events that had transpired in the last few days, see if they were missing anyone and if they could offer some help in searching the area. They wanted us to ask for help and make sure we didn't accuse the gang of anything. We would have to be careful yet try to find out if they knew anything about #25 and #75.

Of the 76 community members remaining, 40 were divided into search parties of eight with specific directions always to have someone partner with them throughout the entire day. They had divided the island up into five grids and, over the next three days, had plans to cover every inch of the island. If these people were alive, this group was bound to find them; even if they were dead, the goal was to come back with answers.

Dr. Linn and the rest of the inhabitants would prepare more huts and beds at the beach and have dinner ready when everyone came back. What had been volunteer dinners, now became required so attendance could be taken so we could assure everyone was back safely and tucked in for the night.

Michael, Val and I went to Jorge's camp. We were greeted the same way we always were, like we were unwelcome and a bother. Peter met us at the entrance and could tell something didn't seem right. He asked, "What do you want? You aren't welcome here."

Val diplomatically asked, "Can we please just Talk to Jorge? It's urgent!" She went on to tell him, "We have news to share and want to ask for help about some things that have come up the last couple of days."

It was about 9:00 am, as far as we could tell, and it looked like most of the camp was still in bed. Jorge and Cheryl came out of their hut and looked "ridden hard and put away wet," as we say in Wyoming.

Let's just say they didn't seem happy to see us and seemed to be put out by our coming to their camp. Deryl came around the corner at that time and took over. He said we could meet in a hut at the end of the camp and that we could talk to him, and he would determine if it was important enough to bother Jorge about. There was no doubt most of Jorge's gang were afraid of him and did everything they could to not piss him off. Cheryl was the only one that didn't seem to care what he thought and was willing not to put up with his shit.

We went to the hut with Deryl and Sam Watkins, the homeless guy we had met earlier. I noticed the two educators we had seen, Marcie Skrinjar and Nancy Schmid watching us as we walked across the camp. I couldn't help feel that if they had the opportunity, they would leave this camp as quickly as they could but didn't feel they could escape without consequences.

Anthony Vacarro, the upstanding citizen from New Jersey, aka possible mob boss, was already in the hut having some coffee. These three individuals were downright hospitable. They asked, "How is everything going? How are you doing, and can we get you some coffee or something for breakfast?"

We were a little surprised but appreciated their hospitality. Being in Jorge's camp is never pleasant, and we wanted to get in, get some information and get out as soon as possible. Michael was succinct, he asked, "Do you know anything about #75 and #25?" He then went on to tell them, "We're afraid they might have been murdered and would appreciate any help you might be able to give us."

Deryl and Anthony asked some follow-up questions about whether we knew when they went missing or any other information we might have. We went on to explain that there were search parties covering the whole island, hoping to find them, but they'd been missing for over two days, and we were definitely concerned.

We made it a point never to accuse the gang of any involvement and made sure to ask if anyone was missing from their group. Deryl listened and said he would talk to Jorge sometime today and see if they could help out in any way and would stay in touch. We did explain our concerns, they already knew about the previous murders from Dave, and we told them these might also be some type of foul play. They needed to be vigilant if they were ever outside camp.

Deryl laughed and said, "We don't have those concerns here; we take care of our own. We don't leave camp and we have very clear rules that govern our behaviors."

He said maybe some of Jorge's gang needed to be part of those search teams, and if they found out who was involved would take care of it effectively. From the way he said it, he made it clear they don't have those type of problems in their gang, people are too afraid to do something that stupid, Jorge would make them pay.

We left with no more information than we had when we first came in. We didn't know if they had anything to do with the missing individuals, but my gut said they didn't. Seriously, Jorge looked too strung out to be capable of having his gang kill two people or helping us figure out who did. It seemed his camp was more into fighting and having a good time than developing a community that could be successful on this island.

As we left, I noticed Dave watching us closely. I couldn't say for sure, but I wondered if he knew about #25 and #75, and if he had anything to do with it. We headed back to camp with more questions than answers and still were not sure if Jorge's gang had anything to do with the missing #s.

That night, none of the search teams had found any evidence of the missing individuals, and it was a pretty sullen camp. CJ belted out some Joni Mitchell ballads and everyone just sort of hung out.

It was boring, and I asked Michael if he wanted to go for a walk. He agreed, and we left the beach and headed into the jungle. I joked, "We're safe because the two of us don't equal 100," he didn't get it till I pointed out that all the individuals that were missing equaled 300.

The single girl, #100, the next two victims, #49 and #51, and the last two missing community members, #25 and #75. He hadn't noticed but did agree it was a weird coincidence. As we walked and reflected on what we knew, we were hypersensitive to our surroundings. Michael was a Navy Seal, and his training had prepared him for hazardous conditions.

Two people for sure and three other individuals might be dead, and we needed to be aware of our surroundings at all times. I was glad I was with Michael and trusted his instincts enough to feel we would know if anyone was following us. As we walked, Michael flashed some signs that we had practiced during the trainings we had; he seemed to be telling me he felt we were not alone. I watched as he veered out of sight to the left and left me walking. I continued to make small talk and as much noise as possible to let him do what he needed to do.

Sure enough, a couple of seconds later, Michael had doubled back and caught Deryl following us. He quickly surprised him, took him down, and put him on the ground. When he called out, I came back and was surprised to see Deryl on the ground, struggling to get up. Deryl was a big boy, and Michael had disarmed him and had him on his stomach, grunting and yelling, "Get the hell off of me!"

Michael released the pressure, and Deryl got up, mad as hell, but aware he had lost this battle. As he gained his composure, Michael asked, "What are you doing?"

We had told him earlier that we were on high alert because of the missing community members, and sneaking up on us wasn't a good idea. He was lucky that Michael didn't do a lot worse to him. Deryl didn't disagree and then went on to explain why he was here.

After Jorge had slept off the previous night's activities, he sought out Deryl and asked him why we had visited. When Deryl first explained, Jorge got really angry and thought we were accusing his gang for these missing individuals. Deryl had assured him that they hadn't accused anyone of anything; they were just trying to find out if we had seen these individuals or if they had become part of our camp.

Deryl knew we suspected Jorge and his group, but he had heard nothing from anyone and that a secret like that wasn't something you found in Jorge's camp. Deryl wanted us to know that he didn't think anyone in Jorge's camp would kill anyone. They had their problems, but killing innocent people was where he drew the line.

Deryl then went on to describe an incident he was made aware of, one that, at the time he didn't think meant much, but after hearing what had happened to our people, he thought he should share. Nancy Schmid, #73 and Ken Denning, #27 had been out looking for food and felt that someone was following them. They couldn't be sure, but they definitely felt that they were being watched. Another couple of gang members had met them in the jungle to report back to camp and said they thought they had heard something and wondered if someone was going to jump them.

I asked Deryl, "Do you know where this happened?' Hoping it might give us some clues.

He said, "Up near the farm we were using. Up where Louis, Don and Jessie lived."

Interesting. Deryl went on to say Jorge didn't feel it was a big deal and said if any of the outsiders, that's what they called us, jumped us, his gang would retaliate, and they would be sorry. At the time, Deryl didn't think it was a big deal, but after he heard what we said, he thought he should mention it to us.

Michael and I both looked at each other and had done the math; #73 and #27, equals 100. We thanked Deryl for the information and told him not to try to sneak up on people; he was too big a guy. He laughed, and I felt we had made an ally that evening and gained some valuable information.

When we got back, I found Paige and asked her if I could spend the night again. She said, "I'm not sure; the sexual tension was pretty escalated last night, and if we don't have sex soon, I'm going to explode."

That's what I liked about her, she was very honest and told you how she really felt. There were no pretenses with this girl, and I found that hot. I agreed, but also told her, "I'm not ready yet. I enjoyed the cuddling, but I'm still in love with my wife, and I'm not sure I'm ready to throw that away."

I did hug her and let her know that if I did decide to have sex, it would definitely be with her. She was beautiful, smart and everything I would look for in a girl out here on a tropical island.

I also joked and said, "Remember you're #2, and surely, you could do better than a #98."

After thinking for a moment, she agreed, and although you could tell she wasn't happy, the compliments helped ease the sexual tension between us. I will have to tell you, though, just cuddling is hard, and I'm not sure how long I can go without having her.

I really did find her extremely attractive and there was a definite connection between us. I could talk to her about anything, and we had a lot of fun, and it was tough not to be with her most of the time.

The conundrum was I also was very much in love with my wife, and the thought of cheating on her felt terrible. I was attracted to Paige, big time, but I was married, and the way I was raised told me that that meant something. It sucked.

I know these were extraordinary circumstances, but I needed time before I could have sex with her and commit to that type of relationship. I had flirted with Kim and Jessica a little, but Paige was the only one I thought about most of the time. I told her I understood if she couldn't wait and wanted to go out and see what else was out there. I was pretty sure she could get any guy she wanted. She told me she liked me, and we had fun together, but she did say she couldn't/wouldn't wait forever, and I needed to decide whether I was going to live in this world or the one we used to live in. It made sense, but I had to live with the decision I made and needed more time. We didn't cuddle, and I slept on the floor and didn't get much sleep as I thought about our relationship and what our next steps should be.

Chapter Twenty-Five: #???? =

The Killer

The first female was just in the wrong place at the wrong time. She had the #100 on her shirt and told me her name was Karen Sheets; she was a stay-at-home mom, had three kids and had no idea where she was or how she got here. The terrain I found her on was rocky and treacherous, and I'm not sure she would have made it out alive even if I hadn't met her. She whined about not knowing where she was, and seemed to have a lot of problems, and really, I had enough problems of my own. I didn't know where I was and had the same questions she had, so I just gave her a quick push and Boom! It was over. After I pushed her, I was intrigued that she was wearing the #100. I had a number, but it was much lower than 100.

I navigated out of the rough terrain and had no clue where I was or how I got there. It was confusing, but over the next few weeks, I found other individuals who had the same questions that I had. I'm pretty good at making friends and had a group to hang out with in just a few days.

This place was different from my last residence. Let's just say I've had my share of problems; I moved from foster home to foster home and never had role models. Most just used me for the money they got from the government, and the older I got, the less interest there was in adopting me. I learned early that to get by, I had to play the system.

I graduated high school, even though I seldom attended and found out that by playing the game, I could get by. The game was simple, be nice, treat people with respect, and when they least expect it, lie, and take advantage of what is offered, then get out of town. I moved around a lot, never stayed in the same place more than a few months at a time. The amazing thing was the more I played the game, the better I got. I started with stealing small stuff and moved up to major burglary. Every time I pulled off a job, I wanted to do something bigger. I learned that by being nice, lying through my teeth and staying cool, I could get away with anything. I stole thousands of dollars off a couple that helped me out and didn't feel bad about it at all. The high I got from ripping people off was exhilarating, and I kept taking more risks.

The first time I killed someone, well, let's just say they deserved it. It was a friend I had that tried to rip me off. When I found out, I went crazy and just shot him. When the police questioned me, I lied, and they didn't have enough evidence to convict me. I got out of town and have been a transient since then. I can't tell you how many people I have killed, but I know that it has become a part of me. It's like a drug; if I haven't killed someone, after a few months, I can't get it out of my head and constantly think about who I will kill and how. I also try to leave just enough information that the police could figure out who killed them. It's like a game, and so far, no one has caught me. By the time they figure it out, I'm long gone.

I can't see anyone here smart enough to catch me, so I've tried to leave enough clues to get a thrill, and each murder I commit, I'll leave more clues. Sooner or later, they'll have to know it is me, but I figure I'll kill at least six more people before I have to deal with that.

I'm amazed no one suspects me on this island. I've killed four others since #100. In each case, I get people to trust me, lure them away to remote spots and use some techniques I've acquired over the years to kill them. The second individual I killed after Karen was Marcus, #49; I had asked him to meet me in the jungle near our camp and snuck up behind him, grabbed his head and twisted hard. I had never snapped a person's neck and tried the technique; it stunned him, but didn't kill him. Then I finished him off with the line I developed that was thin and strong and would do the trick of cutting a person's carotid arteries. #51, Judy, was a bubbly older female that I stumbled on in a remote area and saw her number was #51. I had hidden her body in a really remote area of the island, and wished I hadn't hidden the body so well. No one had found it, and although they suspect she's dead, no one knows for sure. It was a coincidence, but when I killed her, I realized the two numbers equaled 100.

I had killed #100 and decided this would be my calling card. I have always been fascinated with this scenario and decided that would be how I choose my victims in the future. The last people I had made small talk with seemed like nice people; I know this sounds terrible, but I just didn't care. I'm in it for the thrill, and I made the decision to kill in pairs of two that equal 100. It makes the "game" more fun and interesting. So far, I've killed random people I either just met or had very little contact with, but I'm looking to make a pretty big splash with my next victims. They seem to be pretty well known. I've met one of them, he seems like an asshole, and I'll enjoy killing him and his girlfriend.

Chapter Twenty-Six: Something Unexpected

The next morning, bright and early, we came out to find Jorge and nine of his gang in our community. We expected the worst, but Jorge and Deryl stepped up and said, "We are here to help." They had heard about the missing individuals and were there to offer support and look for these people.

To say I was shocked would be an understatement. Jorge looked much better than he had the morning before, and the individuals he brought with him seemed ready to help in any way we needed them. Deryl was there, along with Jorge and Dave, the police officer. We decided Michael and I would go out with those three and search the grid closest to the farm. The rest of Jorge's people could split up and go with other members of our teams; they could choose which group to search with.

I figured this could be a chance for our two groups to mingle and meet. It could be a chance for a thaw in the two groups' relationships. Leaders can lead people blindly, but when the people get to meet each other, sometimes good things happen. I was hoping that if some of Jorge's people saw the type of individuals we had in our community, they would be more willing to work with us in the future.

This development had surprised me so much I didn't have a chance to talk to Paige, but I really needed to figure out where we were going, and I didn't want to lose her.

The search started out awkwardly; other than getting my ass kicked by Jorge, I had never really talked to him. When we went to his campsite, he had always been short and gave orders. Michael and I had never had a normal conversation with him and really didn't know what to expect. I think Deryl sensed this and tried to lead the conversation by asking a lot of questions about the missing individuals and where we had looked.

As we walked, I sensed a different Jorge; he was listening and trying to see what we were all about. He wasn't ordering us around; he sincerely asked, "What are your thoughts on this?"

He continued to get our thoughts about the situation and if we had any idea what was going on. Then he did something Michael and I never expected, he asked, "Do you think the two camps can work together and ever get along?"

We didn't see this coming and pondered the idea before we answered. The silence was awkward, but we hadn't expected this conversation. We did what any good politician would do, we asked him "Do you think we can?"

He laughed and said, "Great response. That's how I always responded to the police when I didn't know an answer or what they were looking for."

We all saw the humor in this, and all agreed we didn't see why the two groups couldn't. In the long run, working with each other would definitely be a greater benefit than fighting and not trusting each other.

This opened the door for Jorge to ask if we thought his gang had something to do with this. It was an interesting question, and I answered, "We don't think your gang is involved as a whole, but we can't rule out members of your gang."

We didn't know, other than the first two individuals, what had happened, and we weren't sure what had been done and, if something had happened, who had done it. There were a lot of questions and if we worked with Jorge and his group, we had a better chance of finding out. It was better than having to tip-toe around Jorge and his gang, and this was a step in the right direction.

As we continued our discussion, we heard a shout-out from Dave; he had found something in a dense thicket around the area we had been farming the other day. We all rushed over and saw two bodies, #25, Pat Vogel and #75, Colleen Gillotti.

Dave was hovering over the bodies, checking for vitals, but it was clear both were dead, and there was little you could do for them. We stayed back and checked the area for any signs of what happened. What we could tell was that both had been dragged there; their bodies were covered with dirt and weeds, and both were white and covered with blood around their neck and upper torso. You could see a black and blue line around their neck. It didn't take a coroner to tell they had been strangled with some type of thin line.

Dave had made a mess of the crime scene; he had moved the bodies when he checked their vitals and had walked around the area looking for clues. If there had been footprints, Dave had effectively walked over them. We all stood in disbelief; we knew they were missing, but had hoped for the best. This was gruesome and brutal and left no doubt we had a mass murderer on our hands. The way the bodies were left made it clear this individual wanted everybody to know they meant business and the community better be fearful for their lives.

Word traveled quickly, and Dr. Linn, Colby and Kim showed up to look at the crime scene. Colby was pissed that Dave had contaminated the area but didn't say much.

Dr. Linn confirmed what we had already figured out, they had died when a line of some type severed the carotid arteries in the neck. Colby decided that he would try to follow the trail left from dragging the bodies to see if he could find where they had been killed.

I wasn't an investigator, but it looked like they had been dragged from the same general vicinity and left Colby and Dave to investigate where they came from and if there was any other information they could find out.

We had known these individuals and determined that we should have a service for them. We would dig grave sights and give them a proper burial in the next few days. We hoped the service and the chance to say goodbye may help in the overall healing process, but also realized the stress and anxiety over what was going on in our community would increase dramatically.

Chapter Twenty-Seven: To Catch a Killer

The rest of the week, people were walking on eggshells. Tempers were short, emotions running high, and people were not trusting anyone. A strong neighborhood watch had developed, and there was a pretty strong system to ensure people's safety. Friday night at the camp on the beach, everyone was talking about the bodies and how afraid they were. Colby was starting to ask everyone and anyone if they had any information that might be helpful; he was hoping the killer had told someone something that was helpful, given some type of clue as to who was committing these heinous acts.

Paige and I shared our thoughts about this person having sociopathic personality traits, and Colby immediately admitted he had thought the same thing, and you could see his mind going into overdrive.

Colby shared he 'was concerned about Dave's carelessness around the crime scene and hoped he didn't have alternative motives to contaminate the area.'

Colby wondered out loud that if Dave had a reason to disrupt the scene, he was the first person to find them and may have left some clues that he needed to get rid of. Over the next few days, Colby would recruit a couple of people he trusted and start talking to all the inhabitants of both groups, Jorge's, and ours. He would figure this out, there had to be some leads, and he would find them and get this guy.

The crowd at the beach was anxious but needed something. An impromptu karaoke session broke out with different individuals and couples getting up in front of the crowd and singing. There was some decent talent and as community members drank some alcohol and relaxed, things started to return back to some sense of normalcy.

Paige and I refrained from drinking and were walking around, sort of keeping our eyes out for anything that might stick out, but everyone was hoping that the killer was done, at least for now, and they needed to unwind. As we walked around, we saw Michael and Kim sitting with Don and Jessica. This seemed like an odd pairing, they didn't have much in common, and we hadn't seen them hanging out before, but Paige and I had observed a lot of things that might not be normal in the old world but found nothing really surprising us in the new world we were navigating every day.

We sat down with this group and started chatting. I listened, and invariably, the conversation turned to who the killer might be. Don was pissed because everyone was looking at Louis, Jessie and him because the bodies were found near the farm. He said, "Just because it happened near our farm, doesn't mean we had anything to do with it."

Jessica chimed in, "I've been up there a lot, and so has Tanvir; we would know if something was going on. We've been up there trying to help the community by farming more efficiently and working on their fishing abilities, and people who were accusing them don't get it."

They did laugh about Jessie. They said, you know, for him being such a great fisherman in the old world, he can't catch a fish to save his soul here." If it weren't for Jessica and Louis, they'd all starve.

I got involved and asked some questions about Louis; I had some concerns from our previous encounters and was curious what their take was. Both said he seemed like a good guy, was helpful on the farm and didn't seem like a threat. I asked some more questions about what he had talked about when it came to what he did before he was "planted," and they said very little. Don said, "He didn't talk much about it and liked farming a lot more."

As the conversation continued, Jessica shared that Jessie had a variety of lines for fishing and that he was continually trying new lines because the ones he was using continued to break. I asked if anyone could get access to those lines, and Jessica said they were spread out all over the camp site and anyone that was at the location could get to them.

Paige and I had honed in on Louis and felt that he had some characteristics that might fit the killer. We talked a little longer, then decided it was time we went back to Paige's hut on the beach. We had a lot to talk about.

The karaoke was winding down, and everyone was making sure the people they were with had a safe way to their hut, and Colby, Bob, Dr. Linn, and a couple of others were keeping a close eye on the campsite. Everyone hoped that there would be no more killings tonight and were doing everything they could to make sure everyone made it home safe and sound.

It was a little awkward at Paige's hut; I didn't know what to say, so I continued to talk about Louis and my concerns. Paige said it sounded right, but a sociopath would be a better liar, and Louis, although he had the means, didn't fit the profile from what she could tell. We agreed I should meet with Louis as soon as possible and ask some follow-up questions.

I was scared, this person was unbalanced and took a lot of risks, and in my gut, I felt Paige and I were at risk. I felt I could take care of myself, and I knew Paige was tough, but I cared about her, and if anything happened, I just didn't want to think about that, and we needed to do whatever we could to catch this guy and keep us safe.

I told her I had an idea to protect us and that I had worked on it after I saw the #25 and #75 corpses, and I would like to see what she thought. I had developed "neck protectors." I had taken some bark from a couple of the palm trees and been experimenting with making something that we could place around our necks. The killer's method of murder was to cut the carotid artery by placing a strong chord around a person's throat and pulling it tight. If we had a neck protector that blended in with our skin, even if we were surprised, the chord wouldn't be able to cut the carotid artery, and it might give us a chance to disable the killer before he realized the chord wasn't working. I had put one on, and pulled it snug. The palm bark was tough, and the chords I had used could not get through to your carotid artery.

She put the protector on; it was a little uncomfortable, but was hard to spot, and you really had to look to see it. Paige said, "That's amazing! How'd you think of that?"

I said, "When you care about someone as much as I care about you, you will do anything to make sure they don't get hurt."

She got these big eyes and they filled with tears, and she repeated, "I mean that much to you?"

To which I responded, "Yes, you're the bomb, and it would kill me to lose you!"

We talked and I explained that she was very important to me and this whole serial killer thing had made it clear that we lived here now! "I love my wife and always would," but I can't be sure I will ever see her again. Right now, "I have meant someone that I have a connection with, and everything feels right." I was old enough to understand that it was hard to find, and I didn't want to let it get away. I learned a long time ago, "When you find someone like that, you better not let them go."

I then explained she was #2, I was #98, and I better lock her down now before she realized what she was getting. With tears in our eyes, we both hugged and held each other tight. We slept together, and it felt right. I still was struggling with my relationship with my wife and this whole new world thing, but tonight, I knew I had found someone who could help me get through a lot of the stuff I was going through and make my life in the new world a lot better.

I seriously wondered what Dr. Phil and the experts would say. For now, Paige and I had an understanding that we cared about each other deeply. She also realized my wife would always be my wife, and that meant a lot. It was complicated, but we were in a unique situation and decided being together was the best option for our mental health.

Chapter Twenty-Eight: The Wife (Vick)

My name is Vicki, I'm #98, Drew's wife. Approximately six months ago, my life was turned completely upside down. My husband of 20 years just disappeared. One day I left for work and have never seen him since. He is not like this; he had just retired, and we were looking forward to me working a few more years, then both retiring and spending our twilight years traveling and having fun together.

We had a great life together; we both enjoyed our jobs, were good at them and had enough balance that we had date nights and took weeklong vacations twice a year to keep our marriage exciting. I admit that I was jealous of Drew when he retired, and was worried he wouldn't find enough to do, but overall, things seemed to be going great. Then, six months ago, he just disappeared.

Then it got even weirder. I started reading on the internet about all these other people that were missing. It started with two celebrities, Jessica Morgan and Cheryl Thiel. I saw on one of those gossip TV stations that both had been missing for about four months. Then, more and more people from all walks of life were missing. I got on the local TV station and reached out to anyone who knew something and left my e-mail, then it all kind of took off.

The Today Show called and had around 15 spouses and/or family members on to share their stories. In every case, the individual had just vanished, and police and local law enforcement had no clues. It was like they just vanished into thin air. It was national news, and we came to find out it wasn't just in America. In over 50 countries, the same phenomenon had been reported.

A day doesn't go by that I don't miss Drew; he was a great husband, and we had a terrific relationship. With all the press and interviews I've done, I've been forced to quit my job, and I have networked with the families of other missing persons, and we've started to try to look for answers. The more we look, the more we find there are no answers. We don't know where they are, and the whole world is at a loss for where all these people have gone. It has taken over the news, and governments around the world are communicating, but still, no one has an answer.

It's been six months, and I can only hope Drew and these other missing people are safe and someday I'll see him again. I miss him so much!

Chapter Twenty-Nine: What Would You Do?

The next day, when Paige and I finally left her hut, we saw Colby had a temporary hut made into an impromptu police station. He had recruited Bob, Brodie, Jorge, Deryl and Hakeem and "deputized" them. Their task was to talk to everyone they could to find out anything that might help determine who was killing community members. They didn't know what they were looking for, but they hoped by talking to individuals in the community, something might jump out.

Jorge and Deryl were going to go to Jorge's camp; they both told Colby they would find out if anybody, including Dave, had anything to do with these killings they would find out. Colby didn't inquire about their methods; he just agreed to let them take care of it.

Paige and I had agreed to a plan where I would go up to the farm and talk to Louis. She and Michael would go up to the crime scene and see if there was anything else to help identify the killer. Michael had some background in military investigations and felt he might be able to find something the others had missed. I trusted that Michael would take care of Paige, and I was going to be nearby talking to Louis, so I felt she was as safe as she could be. I couldn't be with her 24/7, and she was very capable of taking care of herself.

We all walked to the farm together; when we got to the farm, I knocked, Louis answered, and I asked him if we could talk. Michael and Paige continued on their way to the crime scene.

Louis and I talked, and I told him I was working with Colby and was asking community members about what was going on and I wanted to see if he had any information he thought might be pertinent. From the start, Louis seemed nervous. I thought I would ease the tension by asking him to "Tell me what was life like before you were "planted?"

He told me the same story, "He had been a stockbroker, done OK, but nothing exceptional." He then told me he grew up in Dayton, Ohio, lived there all his life and graduated from Dayton University.

He went on to explain, "I got married, had two kids, went to work for a nationally known brokerage firm, and that's pretty much all there was to my life in the old world."

That didn't make a lot of sense. The profile Paige and I went over was of a transient, someone who moved constantly and had a variety of problems in their childhood. When I pressed Louis, he refuted everything we had profiled him for. He had a stable family, did well in school and didn't fit any of the criteria we had discussed.

Louis looked up from his hands and stared directly at me; he said, "I have something to confess."

I was curious and said, "Go on."

Louis told me, "I was investigated by the SEC, and they caught me making illegal trades." He had been good at his job, but he had made a mistake, and he was about to be indicted when he ended up here.

Now, I was starting to understand my misgivings about Louis. He wasn't a sociopath but a decent guy that screwed up and was too embarrassed to tell people. Those were the red flags I was sensing.

I then moved on to what was going on in our community. Louis was still nervous and was evasive when I asked him about how much he had been around the farm. I asked him if he had been in the area where we found the bodies, and he said no.

When I asked if he knew anything about the different lines Jessie had been working on, he got very nervous and started to sweat. He exclaimed, "I don't know what you're talking about," and clammed up.

He wouldn't talk so I changed the subject and asked him about the first time we met. How I hid from him and caught him off guard. I told him I suspected he had set the other two up and was the instigator, and he laughed and said, "I wish." Jessie was the mastermind; he was always getting him to do things like that.

All of a sudden, a light bulb went on. We thought Louis had taken the line from Jessie, but maybe Jessie made the line for fishing and killing. I remembered Jessie telling us that he fished all over and never was in the same place for more than a short time. That fit the profile Paige and I talked about. If that wasn't enough, Jessie was always comfortable telling stories of what a great fisherman he was, but then would tell us he never won any titles, and Jessica, the night before, told us how Jessie never caught any fish.

Didn't we all know a fisherman who stretched the truth and told "fish stories." The more I listened and heard what Louis was saying, the more convinced I was that Jessie was the killer, not Louis.

My questions took on a more urgent tone. I asked where Jessie was, and all he said was, "Out on the farm."

I asked him if he was with Don, and he told me no, "Don went down to the beach."

The more intense I got, the more frazzled Louis got. I started to press, and he told me Jessie had once "put one of the lines around my neck and told me I better be good or he would gut me like a fish."

Louis went on to say that Jessie came up the next day and told him he was "just kidding yesterday and told me he was sorry."

I heard enough, and I took off out the door, heading for the crime scene. It was about a half mile away, and I needed to get there quick.

Michael and Paige had just gotten to the crime scene when they saw Jessie. He approached them and explained he had heard something and thought he would come over and investigate. He had been tending the crops we had planted and was pulling weeds and clearing the brush. He told Michael and Paige the crops were looking great and invited Michael "to come over and check them out."

Jessie was friendly and seemed like he really wanted Michael to see how the crops were doing, and Michael felt obliged to check them out. Jessie knew I had helped plant them and thought Michael could let me know how they were progressing.

Jessie panicked, Michael walked away, and he was alone with Paige; he may never get this good of a chance to kill her again and had to decide.

He left Paige and followed Michael; he was talking about the crops and pointed out the potatoes and told Michael he should bend down, you could almost see them growing. When Michael was distracted, Jessie picked up a rock that had been cleared from the field and hammered Michael in the back of the head. Michael crumpled to the ground, and Jessie headed back to Paige.

She had been looking at the crime scene and was in the thicket and hadn't seen the events on the farm. It had only been a couple of minutes, and Paige was looking at where the bodies had been dragged. Jessie came in behind her and quickly wrapped the fishing line around her neck. He tightened it, but something was wrong; it wasn't cutting into her skin.

Paige realized what was happening and turned and put her fist into his Adams Apple. It caused him to wheeze and cough and temporarily stunned him. Paige started to yell and run towards the farm, but Jessie had recovered and was chasing after her, telling her, "I'm going to kill you, you bitch! And your boyfriend, too!"

He caught up to her, tackled her and put his hands around her throat. He realized there was bark around her throat, and that is why the fishing line hadn't tightened;

he tore it off, got another line out of his pocket and attempted to wrap it around her throat.

Paige was tenacious and poked at his eyes and throat. She was relentless, and did a great job of fighting Jessie off, but Jessie was a big, strong boy and finally got her on the ground and tied her hands. Paige had fought him off for about five minutes but was exhausted. Jessie had to gloat; he started to tell her, "Your boyfriends next. I'll be waiting for him, and I'll make sure he suffers."

As he started putting the line around her neck, I exploded like a rocket out of the brush. I knocked Jessie across the crime scene and kicked him in the groin.

Jessie was dazed, and I wasn't about to stop. I'd got my ass kicked enough to know how to dish it out. I used all the training Michael had taught me and kicked, punched and hit Jessie with everything I had. After five minutes of administering an 'ass-kicking,' I backed off.

Jessie was unconscious, but I had watched too many movies where the bad guy got up. I wasn't going to let this happen. I reached down and picked up the line Jessie had planned to use against Paige, wrapped it around Jessie's neck, and tied it to his hands. If Jessie moved, he would literally cut his own throat.

It was decision time; if Jessie survived, what would the community do? It would lead to a lot of discussion about the death penalty; who would carry out the sentence? If they didn't put him to death, what would they do with him? This was a killer; he didn't show remorse and, if given the chance, would do it again.

He had just beaten Paige and would have killed her if he could have. Paige was still groggy, and I had to make a decision. I set a branch into the ground that was sharp on one end, then took the fishing line off of Jessie. I stood him up and walked him over to the limb, and pushed him onto the sharp side of the limb, piercing his body through his chest.

I walked away understanding a man was going to die, and I could have prevented it, but decided I could live with the decision I had made.

I went over to Paige and helped her walk towards the farm, distracting her from Jessie. When we got to the clearing, we saw Michael and ran over to see if he was OK. He was unconscious, but alive. We helped to revive him and took him to the farm hut where Louis was waiting. Louis and I worked to get Paige and Michael coherent, make sure they were OK and waited for Don to return.

After about 15-20 minutes, Don and Jessica returned after talking to Colby at the beach and immediately became concerned with the way that we all looked. We explained what happened, and all walked to the crime scene.

On the walk, I explained, "I came upon the crime scene, and Jessie was strangling Paige. I lost it."

Jessie and I had battled, and it became pretty violent. Jessie was strong, and we fought intensely, and ultimately both were getting tired. As I was explaining, we arrived, and everyone saw Jessie impaled by a tree limb, lifeless and bleeding out.

I explained, "As we continued to fight, Jessie and I were going at it. I saw the limb and maneuvered Jessie into position and then knocked him onto it."

I could tell Michael had some questions, but didn't say anything and took me for my word. Michael went over and checked his vitals and confirmed he was dead. We agreed we needed to get back to the beach and tell our story and let the community know what had happened, the evidence that we had, and the killer had been taken care of.

Although Michael was unconscious and Paige was too groggy to remember anything, they wanted to corroborate my story; they thought it would sound better if they were witnesses. I stated, "That's not an option. You didn't see what happened, and people would have to believe me, or they could investigate on their own."

I had a lot of internal struggles and was willing to meet this head-on. I didn't want others to be a part of my 'lie,' and I wanted to end this chapter in the new world's book and get on with figuring out why we were here and what we could do to prepare for the future.

Chapter Thirty: What does Due Process look like?

It was late when we arrived at the beach, but a lot of people were milling around, and Colby was still talking to individuals to see if they may know something about the missing individuals. He was trying to see if anyone had seen something out of the ordinary that might have helped him figure out who the murderer was.

Jorge and Deryl had come back and were talking to Dr. Linn and Kim on the beach. When they saw us walking towards the beach, everyone came over to see what was going on. Michael, Paige and I looked like hell; we were all battered and bruised and looked like we had been jumped and beaten up. Colby came out of the hut and hurried down to find out what was going on.

Everyone was concerned and asked what happened; it was chaotic, and there was a tremendous amount of energy and anxiety. We were all tired and beat up, and Don started off the conversation. He explained, "Jessica and I got to the farm and found Michael, Paige, Louis, and I looking bruised and battered." He said, "They looked like hell and seemed disoriented. When we asked them what happened, they told us about Jessie."

Michael went on to explain, "Jessie was showing me the farm and some of the crops and out of the blue, he picked up a rock while I was looking at the plants and knocked me out. I didn't see it coming, and I'm still out of it."

Paige interjected, "I was out at the crime scene, and Jessie snuck up behind me and tried to strangle me. Luckily, Drew had made this neck brace, and I really think it saved my life." She was emotional but continued, "We fought, and Jessie was telling me about the others and the way they all had trusted him."

He went on to tell me Drew and I were next and continued to try to kill me. He had just gotten on top of me and put the line around my neck when Drew showed up. He tackled Jessie, and the two of them got into a fight. I was semi-conscious, and that's all I remember."

I then intervened and took over the commentary. I repeated the story that I had told everyone at the farm and explained that Jessie was dead. I explained as I was talking to Louis, I realized he had seen some evidence of Jessie having some tendencies of the sociopath Paige and I had profiled. He had found a fishing line that was similar to what had killed the most recent victims, #25 and #75, and I realized that all our lives were in danger, especially

Paige's. I took off for the crime scene where I saw Jessie putting the fishing wire around Paige's neck. A fight had ensued where it ended with me pushing Jessie against an exposed tree limb and killing him.

After all that had happened, and everything they had heard, most of the community members were all pretty sure Jessie was the killer and that he was no longer a threat. I looked at Colby and asked, "Can you go up with a couple of others to make sure everything matches up with our account?" I wanted to make sure that people were secure with our account of the story, and we could move forward.

That night, Paige and I went to her hut on the beach. We were dead tired, but the adrenaline was flowing, and Paige wanted to talk about the situation at the crime scene; she had a few gaps and wanted to talk through them. She told me, "The bark saved my life, and Jessie had been confused, and it gave me time to fight back."

As she fought, she saw Jessie go from this sane, friendly individual to a crazed killer. He wasn't used to things not going his way, and she had to continually fight him from killing her. We agreed her fighting back added valuable time to my getting there, and although she was bruised, she was alive, and that was the best news of the day.

She then said, "I was dazed and groggy, but it had seemed that I was in control of the situation, and Jessie was tied up."

I didn't say anything. I just let her finish. She said she didn't remember anything else and asked what happened. I simply stated, "Jessie and I had struggled, and ultimately he ended up dead."

I told her I didn't want to go over the scenario, it was something that I was struggling with, and she would just have to trust me that Jessie would no longer pose a threat to people in the community. You could tell she wanted to ask some more questions but decided to just move on. We were both exhausted and fell asleep in each other's arms.

In the morning, I was met as I was coming out of Paige's hut by Colby, an individual I had never met, and Representative Hix. Colby told me he was going to the crime scene to check things out. Representative Hix then introduced me to the Honorable Joseph Scarpitti, #4, a judge from the 9th Circuit Court of Appeals, the region that covered everything west of Wyoming and Utah. Judge Scarpitti had kept a low profile since being "planted" here, and very few individuals knew he had been a federal judge; Representative Hix had met him, and they had struck up a friendship.

When everything hit the fan last night, Representative Hix had reached out to Judge Scarpitti to get his take on how we should handle this whole situation concerning the murders and the most recent incident. Both individuals said, "We don't have any doubt that things happened the way you said they did, but in the interest of full disclosure, everything should be investigated, and due process should be served."

I got a little pissed, I had just saved the community from a mass murderer, and they wanted to put me on trial? I started to respond when Paige came out of the hut and asked, "What's going on?"

Judge Scarpitti reiterated what he and Representative Hix had said, and Paige totally agreed.

She said, "In the interest of making sure people in the community feel safe, and they are getting the full story, we should investigate and communicate clearly on what had happened. Honesty and fairness should be a part of our community, and it will go a long way in helping convince everyone in the community that the right things are being done."

I bit my tongue and said, "You're right and asked what would you like me to do?"

Over the next few days, Colby investigated the crime scene, and Dave, who had come over to help, interviewed people who knew Jessie. Now that he had been identified as the killer, Don, Louis, Jessica and some others who stayed at the farm had noticed some disturbing qualities that they had just dismissed earlier. He was always leaving the farm and exploring; he never caught a lot of fish, and when he was asked about it always had some excuse.

They also realized he never talked about the old world, they would all be reminiscing about what they did before they got here, but Jessie never really had much to say, and when he did, it was all about his life as a fisherman and all the fish he caught and how he got screwed out of the prize money for some reason.

The more Dave talked to people, the more these people realized how good Jessie was at lying and how dangerous he really was. They all thought he was just a good old boy who liked to tell stories and whom they could trust and talk to. Jessie really was an above-average sociopath, and it was lucky we had figured that out before he killed anyone else.

In the week heading up to the 'trial' I saw a number of Jorge's gang around the beach. Marcie and Nancy, the two educators, were a constant fixture and always willing to help and get involved. Cheryl had come out once or twice and created quite a stir with her striking good looks and body. She had been on a TV show or two, and everyone recognized her. She had kept a low profile while she was with Jorge but seemed more willing to be visible and part of our community. Most of the males in the community seemed to appreciate this.

Although Dave had been a suspect earlier, he seemed to be working well with Colby, and they made an effective team. I even saw Deryl working with Don and some others on coming up with some ways to improve the tools we were using on the farm. All in all, the crisis had helped strengthen an already strong community.

That night, I was on the beach, and Deryl walked by. I stopped him, and we started to have a conversation. He told me the day that Michael and I had come to the campsite, he and Jorge had a 'come to Jesus meeting,' so to speak.

Jorge and Cheryl were always fighting and getting high; most of the people in camp only stayed because they were afraid Jorge would kick their asses if they tried to leave. Deryl told Jorge, "You need to get it together. You're a bright guy, but you're acting like a gang leader instead of someone who cares about the people they're working with."

Deryly continued to tell Jorge, "The outsiders had a problem, and came looking for help, and thought this camp could help. Let's work to build bridges instead of always trying to piss people off."

Deryl was tired of all the shit and had enough interactions with the outsiders; he thought Jorge should give them a chance and offer them support.

Jorge didn't like it, but trusted Deryl and would think about it. That night, Jorge and Cheryl had a major blow-up, and Deryl had seen Jorge take all his drugs and throw them in the ocean. The next morning, he came to Deryl's hut and said that they should go see if they could help the outsiders.

Jorge apologized to Deryl and admitted, "I've been an ass, and the people in the gang deserve to have a choice, and I need to get it together."

Jorge said Cheryl was "great in bed, but a royal pain in the ass, and we are going to have to figure things out, too."

Since that time Deryl had seen a change in Jorge, a change that he was willing to work with the outsiders and see how they could gradually become part of the overall community and figure this whole crazy situation out together.

That conversation was enlightening and gave me hope for our future. That is, if we could get this whole trial thing over with and go back to trying to get some information on the situation we were in and how we could get back to the old world we had come from.

According to the calendar we had developed earlier, we had been in the new world for approximately five months, 150 days, as of Friday. On Monday Judge Scarpitti would convene a hearing on the beach. We didn't have lawyers;

Judge Scarpitti would call witnesses, Val, the lawyer, would ask questions she and Judge Scarpitti had drawn up and the whole community could listen to the answers and draw conclusions about the whole situation.

There wasn't a lot going on, so almost everyone showed up to hear what had happened. It was like the OJ trial; everyone was there, wanting to find out how this whole scenario played out. It was anti-climactic. Val asked questions everyone knew the answers to. Jessie had been a sociopath; all the witnesses had failed to see it until it was too late. Five people were dead, and Jessie had been the killer. He had tried to kill Paige. I, with the help of Louis, had figured it out, got there just in time and, in the ensuing fight, knocked Jessie into a tree limb, where he had impaled himself and bled out.

Colby corroborated how Jessie died, and there didn't seem to be any foul play; it looked like it happened just the way I said it did. Although the trial was a pain, I think it helped ease everyone's mind that there was evidence that Jessie was the killer and he no longer would be a threat to the island, and we could go back to living a normal life, whatever that was in this new world.

Chapter Thirty-One: Back To Normal, But. . .

The first couple of days after the trial were jumbled; everyone was trying to forget the terror we had been through and still weren't completely sure they were safe. The days after that, things started to get back to normal, I mean, as normal as things can get on an island you just landed on five months earlier with 94 people you have never met before.

Eight camps had been established in the surrounding areas. Jorge had kept his camp and was working to make it more accessible to everyone. They still had competitions on Wednesday night and drew a pretty big crowd. It became a little less intense, but I still didn't sign up; I'd had enough fighting for my lifetime. Deryl, Dave, Anthony and a couple of others stayed because they enjoyed the extra-curricular activities the camp provided and had made it their home, although things had toned down since the crisis.

After the trial, Representative Hix and Judge Scarpitti rolled out the Constitution we had developed. A lot of discussion took place, but generally, it was generic enough that no one had any problems with it. My case had established the due process, and most people were happy with their ability to move. There was discussion about:

1. Individuals could be required to work for the "government" in extreme emergencies.

This was put in place if there was an emergency where we needed individuals to work together to work through difficult times and support each other.

2. All individuals were expected to work for the good of the community.

This was put in place to ensure everyone knew they had a responsibility to support each other throughout the community.

Most were unsure what this meant and who the government was that would determine this, but they did understand the reasoning behind it. With eight groups out on the perimeter, it was decided each would have one representative to make sure their views were heard and one at-large representative. There would be an election next week to decide who the three members of the Senate would be, but the only three that had applied were Michael, Representative Hix, and Jessica.

She was a bit of a surprise, but she had developed a solid reputation for knowing what the people wanted and going out and fighting for it. Unless a dark horse candidate emerged, it looked like those three would be our ruling triumvirate.

The farm was about to harvest the crops, and although we had found some of the vegetables before we planted, the idea of plenty of corn on the cob, fresh potatoes, and all we could make with them, and other fresh vegetables that we planted was exciting. Most things were running smoothly, and the various groups were continuing to find ways to make the life we had in this new world as livable as possible.

Paige and I went to a Saturday cookout where most of the community attended. The discussion in most groups revolved around moving forward. We talked about the past; we talked about the last 5 ½ months and all the confusion that had followed and how we had weathered all of the stuff we had gone through.

As always, we talked a lot about whether we would ever see our friends and family, but the longer we were here, the less we felt that was going to happen. There was always discussion about why we were here, and we talked about how everything we were going through seemed like a test of our resiliency and ability to deal with problems.

From just being 'planted' here, to Jorge's camp and the conflicts it created, to struggling to make it in our everyday world, to the murders that took place, everyone, in the back of their mind, felt we were being tested and wondered what was next. Little did we know we would be finding out soon.

Epilogue

The results were in for the American Above-Average group:

Number remaining for the next challenge:

94 remained alive and functioning.

Ability to respond to change and show adaptability and flexibility:

9 ½ / 10

Americans, although confused about the various environments they were placed in, showed the ability to communicate and respond to the variety of changes that they had to navigate. Although there were some problems and questions with the #s on their shirts, Americans ultimately figured out how to work through those difficulties.

Ability to handle and deal with conflict:

9 ½ / 10

Americans overall showed the ability to overcome conflict and find alternative methods to work together to be successful in their daily endeavors. The "gang" presented some problems, but through the use of communication and problem-solving techniques, the Americans successfully navigated this situation.

Ability to "Figure Things Out"

9 ½ / 10

Americans had dealt with being placed in a variety of environments, and different conflicts during that time, figured out they had a serial killer in their midst quickly and effectively and dealt with the variety of challenges they were faced with. They had shown an ability to come together and solve problems together, and that was one of their strongest qualities.

Summary:

Characteristics the Above Average Americans exhibited:

Solid work ethic and is not afraid to spend extra time to make sure something gets done.

Develops real and authentic relationships with others.

Communicates well and listens to understand.

Gets a lot of information and input before they make a decision.

Finds time to have "balance" in their lives.

Doesn't have to get credit for things that are done well.

Always there, on time and ready to work.

Out of the 50 countries that had been 'tested,' the Americans had dealt with the situations they were placed in quickly, effectively, and as a TEAM, and therefore, moved on to the next round. The Americans demonstrated these characteristics to the fullest and will continue to be tested in a variety of ways in the next challenge.

About the Author

Phil Thompson is a retired educator. He was a teacher and coach for over 25 years, then moved into the administrative arena the last 15. During this time, Phil worked to provide support for the students in his schools and worked to find common sense solutions for difficult problems facing the educational system in America. He now is using all he learned in the educational arena to write books to continue to educate.

9 781917 238038